The Rocks

DIMITRIS STERGIOU

Copyright: Stergiou Limited, 2013-2014
ISBN: 978-1-910370-19-3 (Stergiou Limited-Assigned)
ISBN: 978-1494251383 (CreateSpace-Assigned)

CONTENTS

Some critics instead of introduction

The novel was written in 1970 and first published in that same year. It received much criticism from writers and from O'Reilly in that era. It was rereleased in 1992. Here are some brief reviews from major critics and writers of this period for the first edition:

• **Constantine A. Diamantis** (general director of General State Archives): "...The book "The Rocks" has everything. It is poetry and music and painting and philosophy, but it is generally a reflection of the beauty of life and creation. With 'beauty', of course, I don't mean the beauty of Apollo - peaceful and imperturbable as it is in its absolute state close to God, but I mean the beauty that is struggling dramatically, that is fighting with the conflicting forces in order to create and climb a ladder- a ladder leaning on the skies, a ladder that is the route of the human to the Absolute; the so hard to climb stairs to the alikeness to God...".

• **Babis Claras D.** (journalist O'Reilly): "... A meaningful allegory, written in singular style poetic symbolism ..." (extensive review to the 'Literary Night' on June 7, 1970 under the heading "From the place of Christ as the simple life, works of human love").

• Georgios Athanasiadis - Novas (Author, politician, former Prime Minister): "The Rocks is infused with poetry. Congratulations."

• **I M Panagiotopoulos** (philologist and writer): "Are you all flame, creating more and more momentum, dear sir Stergiou. His prose is gradating. His poetry is inspiration. Lyricism and prose mellowed with such generousity...".

• **George K. Stambolis** (Writer): "I would like to congratulate you on your novel "The Rocks.""

• **Takis Chatzianagnostou** (Writer): "... I was struck by the persistent exploration of the part of the hero the truth in life. The search of love, even though it always brings back the feeling of death. After all love is immortal and the dynamic coordinates, the cross-checking balances give meaning to life and its duration in perpetuity. I really liked the symbolism of rocks. I would like to shake your hand. Above all because from your first page until the last you remain faithful entirely to an your own attitude, without concessions..."

SUMMARY

The case briefly

Constantine Ostas, a University professor is spending his holidays at his home village with his family. One very hot noon on August the 13th, he gets his books and archives and lies down in the garden under the shady pergola. There, he is overwhelmed by thoughts that turn into vivid memories and bring him back exactly twelve years ago at the same place.

His memories begin from the day that he, as a graduate of the University, visits the house of his fellow villager Helen, who is a student at the School of Philosophy in the University of Athens and to whom he had been closely acquainted two years ago. Back then a mutual respect had developed between them which eventually evolved into mutual love, but without any continuation. The son of a big landowner of the village, John Kostoula was madly in love with Helen, but she rejected him discreetly. After that John tried to establish relations with Helen's sister, Alexandra, a schoolgirl, who also rejected him. This behaviour of Helen and Alexandra turned his love for Helen into hatred against Constantine when he learned that when Constantine came to the village, he went straight to her house and then went with her for hiking tours to the rocks...

The memories of the professor of his love for Helen, the behaviour of John and his shepherd, (the sly Mitros) and the deep discussions with intense lyricism and metaphor about his love for Helen are covering the first nine chapters of the novel. And so it is a kind of 'boxing' with the past, but in the present!

These memories are interrupted abruptly when the scene of the tragedy at the rocks is introduced - the death of Helen and John caused by falling rocks. Two years after Helen's death, Constantine married her sister, Alexandra, in respect to Helen's last wish that she shared with her father in her last breath, and acquired by this marriage a daughter of ten years, whom he named Helen. The landowner Kostoula donated half of his real estate in the area of the rocks to the church, and the other half - to the village community. Constantine bought his half estate at the rocks from the community by winning a contest a year ago.

In the following chapters the lyrical and allegorical catharsis of the character is revealed. Mitros, chased by his remorse, reveals to the teacher, Constantine, that the tragedy at the rocks twelve years ago was not an "accident", but a plan to assassinate him, which he and John had elaborated.

After these revelations, the teacher decided to divide the land he had bought between the landless of the village, giving ten acres to Mitros, the killer of his beloved Helen! Also, the donated money to the community to build school with the stone from the rocks which he flattened and in their place created a garden...

Symbols and words that dominate the text

There are many symbols that are repeated throughout the text, especially in terms of punctuation:

1. The exclamation point (!) symbolises admiration or satisfaction from a statement or disclosure, confirmation or verification.

2. The exclamation point with three dots (!...): It means the protagonists bode unconsciously, something bad for themselves and others.

3. Three dots (...): It means that the debate, issue or the case will continue.

Also, there are many words that dominate the text with their symbolism:

1. Love

2. Eagle

3. Man

4. Spring

5. Daffodils

6. Dawn

7. Rocks

8. Happiness

9. Life

10. Death

11. Shadow

12. Sound

13. Lyre

14. Hatred

15. Music

16. Darkness

17. Song

18. Hymn

19. Moon

20. Voice

21. Light

22. Joy

23. Time

Finally, the text is allegorical when it refers to people and scenes mostly from Greek mythology that occur over time; lyricism and symbolism; the power of passion and love from the deepest antiquity to the present.

CHAPTER ONE

Memories in the garden of the house
one afternoon in August

Last summer was endless. I will go and lay down under the vines to proofread a new book of mine and to put some order into my endless archive, right here under the arbor full with fruits, just as I was sitting exactly twelve years ago. The night before Panagia, before August 15th, before the festival in my village…

"The rocks, you didn't mind the rocks!"

It was a voice that I always used to hear at this shore. But the voices don't always say the truth. They have their own content and their own purpose. At the height of the rocks I didn't look for their meaning. I just figured out that the they are the foundation of time.

For years now I have been looking at these rocks. I thought that they consisted of one piece, that at their top there was no place to sit, that as imperious and tough they were, they were supervising the shore strictly, digging into the clouds and being all ironic to the raindrops. I had reached their feet where I saw many pebbles that had fallen down there and there were even more of them waiting at the top.

It was a voice that I always used to hear at this ravine.

Until now, the rocks were just one big mass in the ravine. The voice was telling me to find a truth, one value equal to the unknown time. The rocks were a blackboard.

I had to keep walking, because only this means strength!

I was not able to see the signs very clearly - neither positive nor negative. There I would find the truth, that thing that doesn't conflict with reality. Not a thing as small as me - a tiny dot in their shades, a small carpet in front of their feet, just one more worshipper of their height!

I had to keep walking, because only this means strength!

In summer, in the silence and the heath, in the smoke and the furnace of the day, the voices can be heard more strongly and clearly. The day is one colour of time. The shadow of the rocks was growing as the fire circle was becoming smaller near the pillow of the mountain. The waves were running rapidly, they were coming and kissing the shore, they were leaving a trail - like a secret - in its feet and were worshipping my feet. All of us are being both worshippers and worshipped. The rocks are on top of all the rest, they have no limits, their pedestal is big enough and so it is possible for us to erect a fake statue made from soil.

Then I remembered the winter, the seaweeds, the fish. All these three things are circles dependant on one big circle - the circle of time. Life is the sum of all circles, at whose centre we find a bright mirror, a shore that brings together all circles. Now all that is left is the radius of each circle. The circle of life is always seen through a lens. It's never real. If it was real no other circles would exist, no other rocks would exist in the ravine, no waves would exist in the bay. The time is limited. And it is still be possible that the rocks would not exist. Are the rocks not reality? Are the rocks not truth?

Then I felt their shadow pulling me up from my hair, the wave hitting my feet as if it wanted to unglue them from the small pebbles and stones of the shore, to push them away, to make them stronger.

I had to keep walking, because only this means strength!

I was losing the light of the day. And the light is un unknown term that comes out in comparison with two known others - the day and the eyes. And now the whole of God's creation was coming together lightened by the sparkles of the fire sphere and now I could see that in the darkness there would come another darkness - deeper, heavier, thicker; one mass whose joys were hidden by the night, and left without the voice of the eagle. If I could find some light in the darkness, it would undress even more the lie of the present moment. That bright light that was presented to me, I never used it straight away. And if it disappeared in the middle of the way,

I would not be able to move on in the unexpected thick darkness. And this is one unknown light. I was never looking for the truth in the "truth". I could always spot the lie when at the crossroad they were shouting the name of the truth to me. I found the truth at the end of many roads. The rocks were one universal "truth". The voice at the shore was also one truth of the "truths" and one lie of the "lies".

Until now, the only truth is that I kept walking.

I had to keep walking, because only this means strength!

I was still on the road though. One dried stream made me stop. I called it a grave. I saw the ruins of someone's life. It was dried out as if by big and greedy mouths. However, even though they were left wide open from thirst and greed, it became their grave. What is life? Life is the food for one other's life, for a stronger one, and later on - his death. It's one circle - small or big - full with other circles in different colours. It could have only green, red or ocean blue lines. When these lines exist, the rocks don't exist. Then life is a cottage without the shadow of the rocks. I pull out of the inside of my rucksack one very dry and broken plate with a thousand cuts, a piece of soil torn from the dryness. The circles of life are in my hands! It's one shape that looked as if it that never had life, that was thrown in there without a purpose. I was stepping on the circles of life, on its dried tongues, on the dead stream. And my feet sounded like voices, like moans! The skew, gravel, earthy cracked plates broke. I threw one. It broke into pieces. It was a voice born from the earth, the water and the burning heat!

I passed there for the first time six years from now. Back then I was not going to the rocks. I was going to the cottage. The last time I passed through that path was last year in April. Then I left the cottage. It was not my purpose to never come back. I didn't even understand how so many months had passed by. Then the daffodils[1] at the sides of the road were bowing to me hurriedly, as if they wanted to stop my journey and keep me in the ravine.

I remember that I stopped then. I stopped in the ravine that was fading. I leaned on wooden bridge so that I can look at the ravine, covered by the daffodils. One green sheet covered its dried streams, its curls. On the two small hills, the sheep was walking slowly as if they were caressing the breast of a virgin that was bending at this first touch, they were giving life to its bowels, and the ravine was there not knowing what the intentions of those white friends of her were.

Then I remembered January and my 'prophecy'. I 'predicted' the end of the stream, its earthy plates, its dry belly. I liked that ravine because of its fruits, because of the life that it always held in its bowels, that it strengthened and bred with the first sprays in its crops. I 'predicted' the death of the ravine. I 'predicted' that the fruits of the valley would get ripped apart by the storms. The stubbles are hiding the fruits that their death presented to them. For the valley, the death was born, so that the movement could die, so that it could stop their snoring and start the silence. And now when I stepped on it, the passage became more narrow. It didn't think that others will pass standing! Back then I passed the bridge that its arms were supporting. Today, I am walking on its dried organs because I 'predicted' their dryness.

I had to pass, because only this is my purpose!

The rocks were waiting for me. I don't know if the ravine had heard my poems. Maybe it only paid attention only to the poems of the rain. The rain was their food! And I would keep reciting poems even if it was dead!

Water wired, turbid water,

when the winter's gone

where will I find the spring

where the flowers come out

to change your shape

with a bouquet from them

for you to play with them?

A river of wild water

when the summer comes

in the thrown pebbles
of the dried river bed
I will lay down, where the
deep was and where I was fearing for you,
where I was looking at you so cruelly
dragging the stubborness
of the road!

The bridge was useless for me. It looked like ugly bracelets on the hands of a pale, dead, but beautiful young girl; as if she was trying to connect two dead pairs of arms into a hug. In its wooden legs there were many dry weeds, dry weeds that the swollen stream was dragging proudly in the rough winter. Roots, bushes and dry woods were following like captives the turbid water that was leaving in the valley one moan, one voice that scared us as it was coming out of its wild waves. It was the recognition of one random and temporary strength that balls in itself, the shame of an impetuous mood, the waste of the wildness, the result of one finish like this: the real force, life!

In the drunken madness of this force, I recited my poems, knowing that the result of the drunkness has two faces: one for the one who is drunk, and one for those who didn't bend under his urge:

Unable to fight the crops
in the ravine of the waves.
And the red mud remained
in the green meadow.
I was throwing seeds in the soil,
so that it could give me fruits
but the winter left it
with no life in its bowels!
The valley with its wild hair,

the mother of winter,

are you forgetting that in rest,

there is strength?

Are you forgetting that with your withdrawal

in the ridges you will be dragging

weeds and wild thorns

in the mouth of the sea

to throw them?

When you will be disappearing

then strong and rich

my crops will become.

Those were the last poems of the day. With the silence, the darkness started uncovering the sovereign rocks, something like giants in the valley, something like werewolves in the silence, something like black masses in the overspray of the night. My route was very familiar to me. For so many years it was stretching in front of my feet. When I left for the last time, I left there - at the valley with the daffodils - my thoughts that were cutting my bowels as if with a knife and winnowed my dreams in the dried daffodils. I left them in the cottage in the valley, a little bit further than the rocks, in the first light, in the first field, where I was seeding the dreams of my youth, in the first Pilius[2] there for one Colchid[3] with one expecting witch Medea[4].

I would spend there my evening there, where I was spending all my summer evenings, all the holidays. It was not very far from my village. In the middle of around hundred acres of fertile earth I built my cottage for my old age and for the rejuvenation of my thoughts. There you can both feel the joys of nature and see its ugliness in the hours of its bestiality. There, further from the sea, there, closer to the rocks, there, in the middle of the valley, there, closer to the forest. I had to pass seven springs to drink from their water - even now in summer- to hear their gurgle, to hear voices that were coming from the land of the dead. I was in their land. Their border was the stream!

The past, its land, I never denied, because denial was not for me. Even though so many circles passed in front of it, it was not showing denial. The present tried to deny the past, my dreams, the idol. But it couldn't and it ended up humiliated in the feet of the idol.

Eternal idol, rigged always on the same road, that now I walk on through the days and the nights, holding my soul in its hands like Zephyr, I didn't see you sitting at the other side of the reef! And still, you could have been sitting there. Life jumped out of your beauty and with it, as if you wanted to put a bridge between the banks of the ravine, you chose to connect two chaoses. You follow me taking this route so that I can find you at the rocks. There is your place. You follow me everywhere, I see you standing in front of me as if you are scared of my denial. And still you know - you are my idol!

You are staring at the infinity as if you are looking for something that you are not missing. You jump, it seems it to me, to where your reflexion makes you bigger. You grow as you go further, a beautiful world is cuddling in you and in your silence I find the word. When I first heard it, I didn't look to find the meaning in it. From it I asked to give light to the cloudiness. And I always had light! It didn't deny me the rays of the dawn, nor the music of its palms. And this is why I am giving the thing that she gave me when she opened her bud: her aroma!

The clouds couldn't cover the idol, because it had its eyes turned to the sun. The beauty threw lightenings and the rays kneeled down at its feet. They wrote with fire arrows its name in the clouds and covered the temple of the soul. They fitted in the rocks, but their shape could not touch it!

Now, I find it in the path that I chose voluntarily. The voice was not unknown for me. I was going to the rocks, in the valley covered with daffodils, in the cottage I had missed so much. As if the daffodils have become now the shroud of the valley. Death - whosever death - is a misunderstanding of life, the seal of the unworthy life.

The rocks had to die, because they were… death!…

Lucky are the living that in their top grew the sprout of the soul. Then, why do they need the oblivion?

---

1 Daffodils. *Daffodils are a plant that you can see in meadows, but also in infertile areas. The Ancient were planting this flowers next to the graves as type of an offering to the dead. They believed that they were food for the dead and many poems have been written about this custom. The name "asfodelos" has a greek root and means "a sceptre". Artemidorus in his "Oneirocritica" mentions: "The daffodil… omens death only for the ones that are very ill, as I have noticed very often. I am not in a position to explain for sure why this is happening. Maybe because it is believed that the paths in Hades were full with daffodils." Homer mentions one field with daffodils two times during the visit of Odysseus in the underworld and again when the souls of the candidate fiancés were led to the Underworld by Hermes. Hesiod though, describes the daffodils as the ticket of the poor one, without making allusions with the superstitions that connect the plant with the Underworld. Lucian confirms that the Greeks believed that in the Underworld existed one very big field with daffodils. Hesychios classifies the daffodil as an aromatic plant, whose roots, according to Aristarchus, are edible.*

2 Pilius. *A mountain in the county of Volos Magnesia, next to the city Volos. According to the Greek mythology, it was the summer residence of the Gods and the home country of the Centaurs.*

3 Colchida (Ancient Colchis) An ancient kingdom and the area of contemporary Georgia, on the shores of Black Sea. The ancient kingdom of Colchis had continuous trade connections with the Greek world and was a cradle of civilisation. According to Greek mythology, the mythical king of Colchis was Aeetes, who had the golden fleece.

4 Medea. *In Greek mythology, Medea was the daughter of the king of Colchis Aeetes and the Oceanida Idia or Hecate. From her aunt Circe she had learned the craft of magic, which she was using during her whole life. When Jason, the leader of the Argonauts reached Colchis, Medea fell in love with him and used all her magic skills for the purpose of getting the golden fleece. After that she followed her lover. We have to mention that Medea, apart from everyone else, also killed her own children Pheres and Mermeros, that she had from Jason, jumped into a chariot dragged by flying dragons and reached Athens where she had a son Medeus from Aegis. However, she tried to poison Theseus and Aegeus sent her away and she escaped close to her sun Medeus in Asia, in the country which was called Media after her. Towards the end of her life, she went down to the Elysian Fields where she became wife of Achilles.*

CHAPTER TWO

Memories: Elena's visit sets love on fire

The night, as if it wanted to show me the light of the cottage, like a hope for my tired thoughts, rapidly enveloped its creation. I passed the springs that were murmuring quietly in the silence as a complaint, as unknown voices in a familiar place. However, many times I sat in their cooling lap, I bent and I cooled down my lips in their moist mouth, like a pilgrim at their stone altar. It's true that time covers its footprints on its way. Then only the thought remains and it comes out of the mist and the dust stirred by its clatter.

I stood at the last spring where the cottage was. Of course, it kept on gushing, pushing the water in the small yard that it made by itself, cutting the road a bit on the diagonal. My eyes fell on the big window, on the yard with the small bed of vines and, later on, the rocks. I was looking at the spring that was taking out something of its bowels and it was giving it to anyone without difference, in the same way, with the same never ending smile on its calm face. The rocks, of course, had some height, they had some colour, their own shadow, their own pride. And still they were a throne for the eagle.

"The rocks, you are afraid of the rocks now. Shadow of the shadow of the night."

Again, I heard the same voice, the voice I heard in the valley. The rocks were standing speechlessly trying to spread terror with their shadow. With a voice borrowed from the eagle they show off with their massive empty height. Height is the torture of the idea, the tool of the madness, the stool of unhappiness, the khan of cruelty, an anvil where values pound. From it small things become smaller and big things become bigger. The rocks of Caucasus were the stone torture of Prometheus[1]. The crosses were erected at the height.

At the end of the day, the night spreads its net and together with it the sparkles start again their fire workshop. The sparks throw themselves with the hit of the tortured body of the iron and show all together the collected old irons that they will follow the fate of the previous ones that died on the anvil of the blacksmith. The shapes are of no interest for me. What interests me is the fire iron that will go off as it dives into the water. The blisters that come out are its last breath. Later on, the iron is ready to become a tool for work. The night helps for the evaluation of light. The rocks were a shadow. From its anvil, the sparks were jumping until they could reach the valley and then stopping at the cottage. So, up there, something is being tortured, something is moaning under the screeches of the eagle, suffering from the hits of the blacksmith!

You can hear the sound of my steps at the pavement of the yard in the night as if they are accompanying the monotonous voice of the pond in the trees nearby. Messages from the lives covered with a black veil, destined to flutter only at daytime, mixed together with all the other lives of no meaning for the grave diggers. But in the fluttering I never looked for strength, as a grasshopper cannot be an eagle. In their small wings there are no values, because they can be made from wax. And then there is the sun, and then the sea turns into a grave. After all, the fluttering impresses only in the height. What did it offer to the dry rocky earth? Maybe these voices come out only under the pressure of the night? Maybe the night rustling is a song of fate and the timid flutters are the rough reality?

I reached the house, full of many memories. After that was the knock at the door. The door is not a wall made by stone and mud. The door is an entrance and an exit. Its value is not in its colour; its value is behind it. What can I do with the wall that holds the stones when they become even wilder? The strength that has been collected explodes in the foundations. And then the height sags!

"Who is it?"

It was a voice as familiar as my own. Both voices were able to stand the punches that life was throwing at them.

"Constantine Ostas," I replied.

It was like the valley remained speechless, like the house froze and with the crack-crack of the door, one look that reminded me of Lot's[2] wife from the bible, got stuck on me.

"Good evening, Helen!"

Her lips almost stirred as if they were trying to chase away the rust that time left on a piece of unused iron.

"Oh, Constantine!"

"Time doesn't have that much strengh to change shapes. On its way, of course, it leaves marks. Fallen tree trunks, walls covered with grass and bolted voices are its traces."

"You are right, Constantine. Your arrival surprised me."

"This means that you were not waiting for me. And that's why I came! If you were waiting for me, I would be late! Time becomes shorter or stretches if you only press one button: waiting!"

She laughed! We walked down the hall that was guiding to her father, Vassilis Skrakos. Yes, they were steps into the land of the past. The steps are following us in the same place, the same strip. We were going slowly, slowly. Maybe she denied the strip?

"Welcome, Constantine! You left and completely forgot about us!"

This is how he welcomed me, with a wide smile and a big joy.

"Good evening, Mr Skrakos, Mr Vassilis."

This is how I greeted him and I hurried to kiss his hand. Helen gave me a chair to sit next to her father, who was in bed. His pale face and very white hair reminded me of an eremite.

"It's almost two years now, Constantine, my child!"

He stood up a bit in his bed, looked at me with curious eyes and later on moved his hands. I didn't know what he was thinking at this moment. As if there was some kind of knot that was growing in him and wouldn't leave his voice to come out of the depths of this sphere that was pressuring his soul!

"It looks to me that centuries have past since you left!"

This intervention was made by Helen, somehow cautious. After that she looked at me with a smile mixed with joy that was slowly coming out of the past. So she didn't deny its land. She could not deny it!

"You sound like you are angry at me, Helen?"

She looked as if she was surprised. She shook her head as if she wanted to explain what she said. She didn't speak. I guessed that she didn't know where to start from. Mr Vassilis was sitting in his bed and was looking at me with eyes full with both joy and relief! What can you do with words in these occasions? Images are enough!…

"I am going to prepare some refreshments."

Helen stood up and you could think that she was not stepping on the earth! They have wings the moments of life! These are the times when one can feel them, when you can hear the light fluttering. Free movement is the fundament of life. Cages are its death. I couldn't understand the flow of time in such a small space. Anyone would leave its seal. The seal doesn't take all the paper. Later, in general view, all remains the same. Time is moving all things, but they don't fall or they fall, but at their place there are new ones coming. Dragons spread by Jason[3]. Seeding dragon teeth, he was seeding his own death! But at the end, death defeated him! He found strength or they offered him strength? It's the 'something' in life and in death. So the movement of time is not enough. This has been proven. Same images, same symbols fall and never get up, covered only by dust. The story is the daughter of time that is holding a big mirror. Time is a martyr! Time is not dragging things, it has been dragged! Time doesn't have stops. Time doesn't have epitaphic stones as signs. All these are molecules that were standing in front of its chariot and were thrown into the emptiness.

This is what I was thinking as if I knew that my thought would bring Helen's voice while she was placing the refreshments in front of me on a small, circular wooden table.

"So many months have passed."

"As many as the unimportant molecules that were standing in front of the wheels of time." I replied.

"Now I remember what could possibly be important for you! But can I guess something that is of a great importance, Constantine?"

"Of course, Helen!"

"Where exactly did you throw the black stone for it to pass?" askedHelen.

"I don't remember! But… some stones brought me back! One voice that I always used to hear in the valley."

"…Stones!"

Like this, somehow shocked, replied Helen. I was one unexpected guest in the land where I used to live, where I grew up, where I saw the Light of Life. Nothing changed! Time is only mud! For Helen, the world might have had another meaning. I saw it her face. This is why I stopped.

"Constantine, you shouldn't leave us straight away." said Mr Vassilis.

"Tomorrow we will go together at the building." Helen interjected, throwing herself into the conversation.

"Do you remember bushes with the stacks and stubbles?" she added.

"Of course! I remember the dried straws and stubbles, their decay, death, the rest of the earth after their fruits."

This is how I replied. But these words bothered the host and he jumped…

"Everything is 'vanity'!"

"No, Mr Vassilis," I said, "Everything is 'fictitiousness'! One painting with ripened grapes and a watermelon cut in two. They are both hanging from the same nail. Different colours, you see, and art. Life is a big theatre with many actors and parts."

"Doesn't the grave show the vanity?" Mr Vassilis asked, as if to himself.

"No, Mr Vassilis. The vanity is a result of the fictitiousness. The grave is not vanity. The grave is the end of the part. Because then life would be a still, static actor in the hall. Therefore, actors with no roles. Hence, image!"

"I cannot understand this, Constantine!" he said.

"I, when I don't speak, am I an image?"

This is how Helen, who was listening to everything with attention, came into the dialogue, and who was a very good conversationalist just like her father.

"You were always an image! Even when you were speaking you can hear more the… the initiator!" I said to tease her.

"Well then, it's the initiator's fault," said Helen, laughing.

"Then we are both together on the stage." I added.

She hit me on the back. The last sentence filled her with hope, just as before!

"I like this more than the applause. In the applause, the audience finds its grave. The roles are over! The shadows remain!"

This is what I added with satisfaction. The heat was satanic. Even the leaves were not moving.

"Mr Skrakos, are you coming to sit under the vine bed outside in the yard?" I asked.

"It's very hot, my children. We have the Date[4] today. You go outside. I will lay down."

I stood up. Helen with her velvet hand took mine and we went out in the yard, bathed in moonlight, where the arbor was throwing its dapple shadow. There, close to the roses and the stone wall covered with honeysuckle with its intoxicating fragrance, was the usual small table with three chairs. The vines were heavily loaded with fruits that were flashing in the moonlight.

"Where are we going?" asked Helen.

"Anywhere. I would like a coffee." I replied.

"Then I will make two, I will have one with you." she concluded.

I was left alone in the garden bathed in moonlight. The stubbles were bothered by the bells of the sheep, there were barking dogs from the flocks and from time to time the voices of the shepherds and their whistles. The vine looked whit in the night trenches at the top, contrasting as black lines on a white painting. On the right, the rocks - almost in the middle of the meadow - the house is exactly at the road that was leading to the farm and the beginning, at the edge, close to the forest of acorn trees - looked like one huge bunch of stones, made by someone so that they could look around - around at all sides.

"The coffees are ready," said Helen happily.

"So quickly?" I jested, so just to tease her.

"Oh, I put them on the strongest fire! Oh, you mean I was late...'

It was one innocent reaction to my teasing.

"How easily water boils on strong fire and how easily it gets cold when put on cold ashes that once were fire with flames that were licking the bottom of the pot like tongues. And this happens because as a reaction to the drunkness of the boiling, someone was trying to turn cool them down with the same water. Now it moans under what once had made it blush. It's in the boiling that the iron sticks, they say. Later on it gets cold."

"Just like the coffee! In its warmth you feel the joy," Helen added.

"The air is very hot, Helen!"

"When are you going back to Athens, Constantine?"

"I am leaving in ten days. I just came to the village yesterday."

"We can leave together! I have two exams in October to study for. Anyway, you are going to stay for a few days with me!"

"Of course! What do few molecules mean in front of such a beautiful image…"

"Well, I can kiss you then!"

"No one is going to stop you!"

Yes! And then under the arbor, next to the roses, in the moonlight, she kissed me. Of course, it was not the first time. Helen was showing her love to me in two ways: with a kiss and with silence. Today she preferred the kiss. It was one kiss friendly, spontaneous, innocent! It was the seal of one unexplainable joy, why not even a big happiness. Whilst I was looking at her now to look at me in the light, in the movement of her eyes and in her smile, something was shining. No, nothing has changed in the land of the past. Happiness in the land of the rocks! The seed that I planted in the valley with the daffodils grew and produced fruits.

"Tomorrow we are going to the streams, the springs, the rocks!"she shouted loudly and cheerfully "We will leave in the early morning so that the first sun rays can find us at the rocks." she added.

"You are asking for something that comes into conflict with what you are living right now. If it was winter, you would be asking for sunshine in the valley with the daffodils. And now you are looking for coolness! Now you are asking to recreate one morning of April in the land of the rocks."

"I would like us to live again that morning. With the rays, we put the base of happiness, we built the statue of happiness and we wrote the word 'love' where hate had crushed and where I heard your poems and you heard mine. Let's go, Constantine! What are you still thinking about!"

"It was spring back then." I said.

"For me it was winter!… Life in the urge of fanatic moment. And then your rays broke through!"

"I showed up in your life earlier. Since the time you considered my thoughts and my words as hatred."

"In the darkness the flames throw more light at the thing you couldn't see before, the lightnings are the flashes of the storm, the thunders are the opposite of the speechless air." said Helen.

"The 'interest' is hatred; the 'indifference' is love. The 'interest' meets the… indifference and the indifference with the… 'interest'!"

"Your indifference about my interest brought my love for you, for the whole world, while the 'interest' for my indifference showed me the way that leads back to love."

"What is hiding in the 'interest'? The mean for one purpose. In the indifference for the 'interest' the cover of the mean is hidden. In the 'interest' for the indifference what is hiding? Egoism and later on hatred and later on: despise."

With this note of mine, the conversation was 'on fire', as well as our love. I saw it in her beautiful face, in her big, happiness filled eyes, in her lips thirsty for kisses.

"Exactly, same as in love," she said. "Love is a mean for one and only purpose: for the satisfaction of egoism, for the fulfilment of the free hours…" she added.

"Passion grows together with lust; love grows on the grave of lust. Then we talk about love. Then we reveal passion," I added.

"How can we find the real purpose, Constantine?"

"In the 'mean'."

"And the mean?"

"In the 'interest'."

"When does the 'interest' die?"

"When the 'mean' stops being useful."

"When does the 'mean' stop being useful?"

"When it didn't manage to make the bed for passion!"

"And what about love?"

"When it finds itself at the same place but through other routes! Then it is the same with love. Then it dies as well and therefore it was not love!"

"So love never dies?"

"Love never dies. Love grows and becomes bigger with the physiological harmony of the person. Then we have the equation: Love equals human!"

"Yes, love doesn't die. Everyone is just trying to kill it!"

"You forget that there are also very harmful insects sitting on there."

"Oh, Constantine! How many times do the bees appear?"

"They will die with her sting, with their hatred…"

"I remember when you were sitting on the rock and you were looking at the meadows and the faraway shore. I remember your poems. I will recite them to you now:

I didn't say anything. Time took its prow and with its paddles started hitting the waves that wanted to swallow it. The flames surrounded the idol, ready to melt it with their strength. And so there were many, many paths, as many as the flames. My tongue got stuck to my palate. The weight of my hands was pulling my body to the ground so that it can get more strength from the rest. My eyes were diving into the dance of her eyes. She hadn't lost anything from what they have given to her. I could hear a voice that was warm and clear as gold, strong as the sound of the bell. The same idol, the same spring. I saw in the water her silhouette. It was not silent. It talked to me as before. What am I waiting for! The idol was decorated with rose petals and sprinkled with gold from the bees.

"Don't pay attention to the sweetness of the words." I said.

"No, that remains of the kneading of life."

Yes, Helen's answer was from a voice from the land of the past. It was exactly what we said that morning.

"You are shining more now, Goddess, in your flames. Your pedestal is red like the gift from my heart!"

"You are flinching, Constantine?"

"I got lost, Goddess, in the chaos of your world. And still, I find your words in the path, in the same path!"

"Constantine, there is no unknown path in our happiness. What meaning does it have that we are covering it with a wadding. Wherever we go, the strength of its fragrance will pull us and we won't lose its name in the haze, we won't mistake its image in the darkness."

"My Goddess, I didn't deny you by choosing another way. I was just testing to see if I would find you again if I do this circle…"

"In the land with the daffodils, at the rocks." she added.

"The voice in the ravine was right. The one that was always telling me to pay attention to the rocks."

"Yes, in the land of the rocks, when the sunbeams touch the mountain," I added.

"The world was always looking at the rays of the dawn. I could see the first smile of the day." she said.

"So that it can end with one bitter smile when it gets dark, Helen."

"Constantine, the recognition of the good, the kind, the immortal, it's a trial. The twilight is bitter for those whose morning smile did not survive the rest and the heat of life. The white clouds at the horizon show the sweet smile of life that was all sunshine. Sunshine, because it survived and spread the grey winter clouds. The essence of life. It starts from the green meadow, it passes through the rocks and if it comes back, it will find spring again. The essence of life is physiological harmony, peace, serenity."

"And the levelling of the heaviness."

"Ah yes, Constantine! In the stone mass, we ingrained the word 'hatred'. It has to get mixed with the ruins, to become a ruin, to disappear."

"A spheric pebble that doesn't stay at the same place, you fall to the bottom of the sea, beneath the light. A mass with different colours that stops the light for a moment. This is hatred."

"How in the dance of thoughts your eyes are taking part, how in the dance of sun rays of the soul their value shows?"

"The dawn is the filter of the evening thoughts. It's the smile for the thoughts that jumped from the blurred vision of the twilight. The dawn, every dawn, clears the evening ideas and tries to find the values. We are smiling at the ones that were served so that the evening can pass, to hold the evening in cages made only for darkness!"

She looked at me strangely. I understood her thoughts. In the moonlight her hair looked like gold, it was covering her shoulders and was making her beautiful face look even sweeter. In her beautiful eyes I could see a shore that was hosting an Argo[5]. She didn't speak. She was sipping her coffee, came a bit closer to me, she took both my hands and held them tightly, caressed my hair, brought her eyes next to mine as if she wanted to read into them.

"You are right, Constantine! The dawn is the filter! You need it, darling! I need it." she whispered.

"It's a trial of the kneading of life,"I said, making a turn.

"How in your hands the world is moving and shaking, how in your thoughts I can find mine?"

"In my thoughts I find the truth. Yes, the truth. I showed it to you in the morning, it comes out in the morning. This is the filter. In voices you can find lies, on the top - the abuse, in the bottom - the whole world that moans from the rain that they throw in its eyes. Then, it's the shore's fault because of its storms, its fish, its… abysses…."

"Constantine, the evenings want to live. Their food are the memories."

"The evenings are smoke from the thoughts that come out from an altar." I continued.

"From the altar of the soul."

"From the altar of the soul that covers it with murders and sacrifices to inexistent Gods, inexistent values, inexistent joys, and inexistent goods. The murders are not atonement. They are the 'mean' so that the altar of the human soul can be covered, can moan under the heaviness, can burn and torch together with the victims that thought that they are… mortal!"

"Exactly!"

"And what if the morning thoughts and ideas face the twilight?" she asked.

"Then they are not real and worth. Everything is falling apart and there is only one 'Love one another' left." I replied.

"Is this a real altar?"

"Yes! On it are punished all the victims as murders not of love, but of hatred. This is the pure thought. The rocks are an altar, for sacrifice for the God of hatred. The 'Love one another' is the 'mean' for the sacrifices…"

"However, the altar on which happiness is built is full with lightnings. It's the only altar on which humanity is relying. Then why do we need these rocks, these stone masses?..." she asked herself as a prophet.

"Because there is no humanity, darling. Blurred purposes, injustices, blood, disappointments start from there and end in pain. One idea with many faces. Different for everyone. Whatever works. The usurpers of human weakness are strong. Their voices are the swish of the imbalance. The voice of the eagle in the rocks, the fear of the other… voices!"

"What about the crickets we hear at night?" she asked.

"Helen, they are a small complaint of the darkness. The strange thing is that we hear them in the darkness. They are a proof that it is getting dark. What can you do with the moonlight? Light was given to you, so that you don't fall from the rugged paths. We need it! Apart from that, it's also the habit. We are so used to that repentance that it 'creates psychological conditions' as Aristotle said!"

"The morning is coming though, look."

"For us, yes. For many it is just a repentance and a circle of morning and evening moments."

Quite a long time had passed. It was almost midnight. One minute to twelve. I looked at my watch.

"What time is it, Constantine?"

"Twelve."

"We are waking up early tomorrow morning. We need to go to sleep."

"I will lay outside here in the yard." I suggested.

"Then I will sleep here as well!"

"Whatever you want." I added.

"It's very hot inside." she added.

"Are you not afraid of the mosquitoes?" I asked.

"We are going to use some mosquito repellent." she said.

"Now I understand what you mean by repellent!"

"If there is the repellent, we don't even need a mosquito net."

"Ok, ok, then go to sleep without any mosquito-worries!"

"With a kiss though?"

"Would you like something to eat?" she asked.

"No, thank you. I am not hungry at all. I ate in the afternoon. We should just prepare something for breakfast."

I sat by myself in the yard. The moon was still spreading its light all over the world and covering the nudity of the rocks. I didn't want to go on with my thoughts. I let myself free. I looked around without a purpose. Nothing had changed. Everything was just as I left it. One world that was hiding its face. It looked as if the cottage was hiding the real world inside of it. The land of the past was holding me in its hands.

The voice of the shore was telling me one truth. I wouldn't find it in the rocks. The clue I took from Ariadne from the cottage. It was Helen! My Helen! Helen, who got the first frisk next to me. I signed that on the map and I gave it to her. All these were showing love for the world, for life, for humans, for me.

"My father is sleeping. He is feeling more relaxed here now in peace and the joy you gave him tonight!"

I realised that it was one sweet pretext! Helen wanted to be next to me…

"It's time to rest now," I said "Mr Vassilis is a very bright person," I added. "I am not hiding it - I would sound ungrateful- that he helped me to stand up when the North wind was blowing wildly. He gave me the frames in which I had to move and the bases to build. He was always telling me that famous quote of Menander[6], 'The human is such a sweet thing, when he is a human'."

"His joy since he saw you is indescribable. He was always asking about you and also worried about your absence." she went on, showing her wish to be next to me all the time.

"I was worried about you as well, Helen."

"With your absence and your disappearance! I know, you would say that you were very busy. It doesn't matter. We will talk about it tomorrow. Let's say goodnight now."

"Goodnight, darling."

Then the breeze started blowing a little bit. One cool wind was caressing our faces that were right next to each other. She was looking at me silently as she was lying in the bed. She could feel the joy together with the happiness, as I could feel her happiness in my own dream. This is probably what she was thinking when she was smiling in her dream and the sleep was sealing her eyes, but not her lips. It is the eternal smile of happiness that comes out of harmony. The fake world disappeared in front of her, passed through my eyes and dived in the sea of eternity!

---

1 Prometheus. *According to Greek mythology he was a great protector of the humans, the God of culture, the one who was always helping them even through sacrificing himself. Two times he became the reason for the creation of the human race. The first time when he became the reason for the creation of the human race was when the Earth was destroyed from the Titanomachia and there was no life on it. Prometheus, with an order from Zeus, took earth and water and created the humans. Later on, as he saw that they were living in the wild, he gave them, secretly from Zeus, the fire that he stole from the Gods, hidden in a basket. With his advice, humans learned the power and the usage of fire, they made inventions and became so developed that even Zeus was afraid of them. For the second time Prometheus saved the human race from disappearance when Zeus sent them the Cataclysm. After the stealing of the fire, Zeus seriously became afraid of Prometheus and decided to send a revenge to him. He condemned him to a horrible punishment. He ordered to Kratos and Via to catch him and with unbreakable chains, to tie him to a mountain, Caucasus. Then an eagle was coming every morning and eating his flesh and liver that every night were growing back. This torture would be eternal, if once Heracles hadn't passed by. Angry by the inhuman punishment of the saviour of the humans, he killed the eagle and freed Prometheus.*

2 Lot. *Lot was a son of Arran and a nephew of Abraham. In the New Testament he is mentioned by Jesus, who mentioned his wife as a negative example, as she didn't listen to the order of the angel to not turn her head back to see the destruction of Sodom and turned into a pillar of salt...*

3 Jason. *A hero, according to Greek mythology, who was leading the Argonauts.*

4 Date. *A very ancient method of forecasting the weather for the next year. The procedure was very easy: You observe the weather for 12 days in August from which each day represents each month of the next months. For example: the first day is going to tell us what the weather would be in August, the second - in September etc.*

5 Argo. *The ship of the Argonauts leaded Jason from Colchis, that was built by Argos, the son of Frix, from which it took its name. It was made of wood under the instructions of the Goddess Athens. It had 50 pedals and at the prow it contained one piece of the sacred talking timber of Dodona.*

6 Menandrus. *Ancient Greek dramatourge, representative of the New Comedy. He was born in 342 a.c and died in 291 a.c.*

CHAPTER THREE

Memories: Deep dawn
on the way to the rocks

"Constantine, the night is gone. The morning is greeting us in the garden with its aromatic honeysuckles."

"My queen, I heard the roosters from your towers. We need to leave. Mrs Rini[1], why are you looking at me like that?"

"Darling, what is the dream that my eyes are stopping? How sweet is your dream in the sweetness of your sleep, that becomes sweeter with the crowing of the roosters? Which smile did you choose from the morning light, from the browning of the beautiful girl?"

"Yours, darling, that is like the Morning Star!"

She covered me even better - it was a bit cool - and I felt double warmth as her hand was caressing my hair. My eyes were opening slowly and she was sitting next to me, who knows for how long, and she was looking at me as if she was keeping me company during my last hours. However, now they were blossoming, bringing as well the fruits of life, the essence of life together with the sunbeams. Two smiles created and decorated by the dewdrops that were dripping from a rose mouth. Her voice was like the musical morning chirping of birds that were flying from their nests and were praising, what else, their happiness!"

"Constantine, are you going to tell me the dream you were dreaming when I spoke to you?"

"It was not a dream! It was something in between dream and reality. Have you heard about the king Aneliagos[2]?"

"You haven't told me that."

"Ok then, I will tell you the story, exactly as I heard it in the area of Aetoloakarnania, in the land of Tricard, as the king was called. It's worth listening to. There is the tradition that has its roots in the beginning of the centuries, connected to the ancient city of Oiniadon[3] that today is located in the village Katohi[4] today in Aetoloakarnania."

"Are you going to tell me this story while we are drinking our coffees?"

"Ok. What time is it, Helen?"

"4 a.m. sharp!"

Mr Vassilis had just woken up as well and was sitting on his bed. He was listening to the conversation, the preparations of Helen and was worried about the dawn.

"What happened to you, children? Maybe some annoying insect bit you in the garden?"

"No, dad! We are getting ready to go to the ravine and the rocks." replied Helen.

"Where is Constantine?"

I went to his room, I greeted him and caressed his snow-white hair.

"I envy you kids. It is glorious the August morning. If you find Mitros, please remind him about the lamb. There are three days left until August the fifteenth. Now, while Constantine is here, we will roast it…"

"Ok, dad. Don't get up now. It is too early yet."

"When are you coming back, Constantine?"

"In the afternoon, when it's cooler."

"Did you at least take something to eat?"

"Yes, dad. I prepared a lot of food."

The coffee was ready. We sat around the table.

"So, 'Trikardo'[5]"

"One is enough! We are leaving now. It is half past four. At half past five the sun is coming out. We have one hour way in front of us. I will tell you the story on the way to the ravine, on the way to the rocks."

"Ok, Constantine!"

We were ready. We took our stuff, whatever we needed for hiking, we said goodbye to Mr Vassilis and we left.

"Have a good journey, kids, good journey!"

This is how Mr Vassilis' voice was accompanying is until we heard the sound of the closing door.

"We will 'cut' some walking poles from the bushes so that we can reach the rocks sooner,"said Helen.

"Helen, we came back from this path. Let's go!"

We were walking slowly. The grass was dripping from the morning coolness and in their green and crystalline leaves you could see their morning beauty. In the morning they would have their heads down to earth, complaining, but also shy about their ugliness and with their dry stalks to hide life in the soil. From the many waters that are running all the time, the soil is damp. The small trenches are hidden by the big stubbles and the morning glories. We took the path from the ravine and we got to the shortcut for the small lake. We had to carry on straight ahead and walk down the hill. Our feet, as if the road was pulling them, were following. We were hiking down jumping, running and singing. We found ourselves at the bottom of the hill and at the beginning of the lake. In the easy things you can only find tasteless satisfaction. It looks good only when it has the others' attention. In the descent you are waiting for the victim to fall in the absence of a hug! Up the hill, where the breath stops, the fire of wish starts. We sat on the stones. The sunrise was not yet to be seen. Its messages though were coming out slowly, one by one. There was, you see, the ascent.

"Aneliagos, why are you still sitting? Your enemy is coming! That was the most intense message!"

"I can see that you are very thoughtful today, Constantine! What is happening to you?" noticed Helen.

"If the thoughts are missing, then truth will run away!"

"Yes, you are right, Constantine. Are you going to tell me the story, the tradition, the myth about Aneliagos?"

"Of course, because now we don't have to walk down the hill. The easy way for the feet becomes difficult for the thought to get to the dark place of the soul where the truth is hidden. The mud that is covering it is of no importance. This - the truth- doesn't rust. The light that you hate kills whatever you are hiding. You cannot hide it anymore. And this is how it will scream "You have defeated me"[6]!"

"I can't wait to hear about it, you should explain to me of the myth of Aneliagos in detail." insisted Helen.

"Let's go on then. Let's sit for a while before the first spring."

"Let's go!"

I held her warm, velvety hand tightly and we started hiking. She was looking at me, expecting for the beginning of the myth.

"I can see, Aneliagos, that all of your three hearts are… made from stone," she said, teasing me.

"The good thing is not in the plenty", I replied.

"Come on, Constantine, start the myth!"

"Ok then. There is a story in Aetoloakarnania that in the Oiniades - an ancient Akarnanian city - lived the king Trikardo. Today, the castles that have remained still carry the name 'Trikardo'. They have one certain magnificence and provoke the fear in the visitor, as they are hugging the hill covered with asfako bushes[7] and with their silence it seems like they are a reminiscence of the moments stacked in the chariot of time and in its turns that throw faded shapes. At the anchor of the shore - when the water of oblivion had licked it - you can see the traces of one force that later has become a myth! Something has to happen at these places. The myth covers and uncovers it! The myth is always like an ostrich! The epoch of the Enetokratia. The fates were judging Trikardo in three days. In the three armies, death. Three roads for three days, for three hearts! The apotheosis of the number '3' in the Greek literature by Homer until today. Pythia in three dimensions of her tripod. On it the smokes are leaning. The sunbeams as well. The following poems were heard form the tripod:

God-sent sunbeams, your thread they will burn,

Parents of parents of a fumed

generation,

at your iron gate

the acts of pity

will melt.

Trikardo was punished. His punishment was in the depth. In the height - truth has been tortured and the height dies in the depth from the light!

Locked in the sunless basements of the palace, Aneliagos was waiting for the darkness. Only then he could see the… nature! Only then, when darkness was falling! In the darkness he met the queen Kira-Rini, who was living by herself, locked in her palace, in Plevron[8], an ancient city in the area of Messologio. You can still see the ruins of this ancient city on the left from the road, between the Aetoliko and Messologio at one hill on the road to Antirrio. They fell in love madly. Oh, Aneliagos was quenching his lust in Kira-Rini's bed and Kira-Rini was lighting her flesh in the sunless body of Trikardo. But the light! The light that comes out together with the dawn was also the enemy of lust. The roosters were crowing. Voices that were coming out of the subconscious and were stopping at its gate, while it was closing quickly so that the sunbeams of the conscious would not come in. The night was at its end, when lust was burning at the sunless palace…"

"You see, he was in love." interrupted Helen.

"Just like Kira-Rini," I said.

"So it was mutual love, Constantine!"

"A contemporary definition of love for incompetent people..."

"So this definition doesn't exist?"

"It's a useless accessory for so many other things. Passion is the wish to possess some 'good'. The 'good' in this case is the physical pleasure - clearly biological - and the satisfaction of the success of the 'conquest'. For this reason, many times, love- passion, lust- become bigger the bigger the difficulties are. And then we come to egoism. It is the enjoyment of the beautiful aesthetically. But as soon as this 'beautiful' disappears, attraction disappears as well. It is what Darwin calls 'natural selection'."

"Constantine, is love the 'mean' to enjoy the 'beautiful' and not to find the right thing and the truth?"

"Love is a stranger to both of them. Because then you reach knowledge. Da Vinci said "Whatever you know better, you love the more" and that "The big knowledge gives birth to the big love". If passion is like a 'mean' for knowledge, and if the discovery of truth and the happiness of the good remains standing, then it brings us to the wings of love of all humans. Then we find the high and the beautiful, the good and the true. Then passion becomes a hymn of love that starts from the bodily image, goes through the flesh and reaches the clear skies of the soul, as Solomon chants in 'The Song of the Songs', which is the most beautiful of all songs, the wisdom of all wisdoms for the passion and lust and the desire for the one that is away from the lover. It shows everything that we have discussed until now in a lyrical and melodic way, but also before, two years ago, here in our village. Because 'The Song of Solomon' is the longing of the human soul to become one with the creator and its own essence. It is one hymn of love:

"Let him kiss me with the kisses of his mouth:

for thy love is better than wine.

Because of the savour of thy good ointments

thy name is as ointment poured forth,

therefore do the virgins love thee.
Draw me, we will run after thee:
the king hath brought me into his chambers:
we will be glad and rejoice in thee,
we will remember thy love more than wine:
the upright love thee. "

"This is one part, darling, of the first book, in which the woman says to the man…

"And I will go on, darling with one part from the same chapter, when the man says:
"If thou know not, O thou fairest among women,
go thy way forth by the footsteps of the flock,
and feed thy kids beside the shepherds' tents.
I have compared thee,
O my love, to a company of horses in Pharaoh's chariots.
Thy cheeks are comely with rows of jewels,
thy neck with chains of gold.
We will make thee borders of gold with studs of silver. "

'I will go on, Constantine, with a part from the same chapter where the woman says to her lover:
"While the king sitteth at his table,
my spikenard sendeth forth the smell thereof.
A bundle of myrrh is my wellbeloved unto me;
he shall lie all night betwixt my breasts. "

'And now I just can't stop anymore,' I said, 'Here is one more part where the man says to the woman:
"Behold, thou art fair, my love;

behold, thou art fair;
thou hast doves' eyes."

And Helen continued with one more line:
"Behold, thou art fair, my beloved…"

Later on I reminded her of one more extract of the fourth chapter:
"Behold, thou art fair, my love;
behold, thou art fair;
thou hast doves' eyes within thy locks:
thy hair is as a flock of goats, that appear from mount Gilead.
Thy teeth are like a flock of sheep that are even shorn,
which came up from the washing;
whereof every one bear twins, and none is barren among them.
Thy lips are like a thread of scarlet,
and thy speech is comely:
thy temples are like a piece of a pomegranate within thy locks.
Thy neck is like the tower of David builded for an armoury,
whereon there hang a thousand bucklers,
all shields of mighty men.
Thy two breasts are like two young roes that are twins,
which feed among the lilies.
Until the day break, and the shadows flee away,
I will get me to the mountain of myrrh, and to the hill of frankincense.
Thou art all fair, my love;
there is no spot in thee.
Come with me from Lebanon, my spouse, with me from Lebanon:
look from the top of Amana, from the top of Shenir and Hermon,
from the lions' dens, from the mountains of the leopards.

Thou hast ravished my heart, my sister, my spouse;

thou hast ravished my heart with one of thine eyes, with one chain of thy neck.

How fair is thy love, my sister, my spouse!

how much better is thy love than wine!

and the smell of thine ointments than all spices!

Thy lips, O my spouse, drop as the honeycomb:

honey and milk are under thy tongue;

and the smell of thy garments is like the smell of Lebanon.

A garden inclosed is my sister, my spouse;

a spring shut up, a fountain sealed.

Thy plants are an orchard of pomegranates, with pleasant fruits;

camphire, with spikenard,

Spikenard and saffron;

calamus and cinnamon, with all trees of frankincense;

myrrh and aloes, with all the chief spices:

A fountain of gardens, a well of living waters, and streams from Lebanon.

Awake, O north wind; and come, thou south;

blow upon my garden, that the spices thereof may flow out.

Let my beloved come into his garden,

and eat his pleasant fruits. "

"Can I continue the hymn of love with one extract from the fifth chapter with the "psalm" of the woman to her lover?' asked Helen:

My beloved is white and ruddy,

the chiefest among ten thousand.

His head is as the most fine gold,

his locks are bushy, and black as a raven.

His eyes are as the eyes of doves by the rivers of waters,

washed with milk, and fitly set.

His cheeks are as a bed of spices, as sweet flowers:

his lips like lilies, dropping sweet smelling myrrh.

His hands are as gold rings set with the beryl:

his belly is as bright ivory overlaid with sapphires.

His legs are as pillars of marble, set upon sockets of fine gold:

his countenance is as Lebanon, excellent as the cedars.

His mouth is most sweet:

yea, he is altogether lovely.

This is my beloved, and this is my friend, O daughters of Jerusalem."

"One more extract from the seventh chapter and then we have to stop, because we got distracted by the 'Psalms' and we 'abandoned' Agiliagos," I said:

How beautiful are thy feet with shoes,

O prince's daughter!

The joints of thy thighs are like jewels,

The work of the hands of a cunning workman.

Thy navel is like a round goblet, which wanteth not liquor:

thy belly is like an heap of wheat set about with lilies.

Thy two breasts are like two young roes that are twins.

Thy neck is as a tower of ivory;

thine eyes like the fishpools in Heshbon, by the gate of Bath-rabbim:

thy nose is as the tower of Lebanon which looketh toward Damascus.

Thine head upon thee is like Carmel, and the hair of thine head like purple;

the king is held in the galleries.

How fair and how pleasant art thou,

O love, for delights!

This thy stature is like to a palm tree, and thy breasts to clusters of grapes."

I said, "I will go up to the palm tree, I will take hold of the boughs thereof:

now also thy breasts shall be as clusters of the vine,

and the smell of thy nose like apples;

And the roof of thy mouth like the best wine for my beloved,

that goeth down sweetly, causing the lips of those that are asleep to speak.

I am my beloved's, and his desire is toward me."

"And so we are coming back to the myth of King Aneliagos: In the castle of Trikardo in Apolokarnania, according to the tradition, the myth, was living one handsome young man, Aneliagos, the firstborn son of the king of the county. When he was still a baby in his cradle, he turned off the light of the oil lamp that his father had placed and the fairies cursed him to live forever without being able to see the light of the sun. If that happened… he would die! And this is how they named him 'Aneliagos' – 'the one without a sun'. Every evening though, when the sun was setting, he was going out of his castle, going across a big river (obviously Acheloos) with his white horse to see his lover, the Lady-Rini (Irini). She was living in her own castle close to Messologi. This kept happening for a really long time. And so, long before the sun rises, Aneliagos was going back to his white horse and by the same route, he was going back to his castle in Trikardo. However, Lady-Rini, because she wanted to 'possess the good forever' according to the Socratic perception of love, she was deluged by bad thoughts: "Why is he coming only by night?", she was asking herself. "And why is he always leaving before sunrise?" she was saying with suspicion. "May be he loves someone else, my king?" she was wondering, poisoning her mind. And in this cases, as we have repeatedly noted in our conversations, we have to look for the truth at any price. And so, she gave an order to her trusted servants to slaughter all the roosters in the area! Aneliagos went as always to visit Lady-Rini with his horse and spent the night with her. But the roosters didn't crow and this is how he lost track of time. When the dawn was there, like now, Aneliagos got up quickly, jumped on his white horse and galloped to meet his enemy, the Sun! He passed Acheloos, but the sunbeams found him just in front of the gate of his castle. And he fell on the ground."

"Did he die straight away?"

"He opened his eyes and looked at the sun while he was floundering like a fish; he stretched his arm as if he wanted to hug the sun! His eyes were throwing sparkles that were becoming one with the sparkles from the sun and in front of him all the dark angles of his souls were full of light. He shouted with a voice that sounded like it was hiding a great pain. Let me remind you my poem that is dedicated to the myth of Aneliagos, oh, please let me recite it:

Enjoying

without joy

for years

I needed your colour

to see

hidden in the sunless

castles of Oiniades.

Oh master, born at dawn,

my enemy, that makes my soul tremble,

now in the sand

of the shores of my life

you stabbed my sunless body

with your burning arrows.

The iron gates

open

are waiting for you

to come in and mow

your steps made

in the dark,

to turn on lamps

that have instead of oil the night

instead of wick- my life.

I'm burning out."

After that Helen was not talking at all. She was standing, deep in thought, and then sat at the rock at the spring that we had reached in the meantime.

"Do you want to sit for a while, Constantine?"

"Of course, this is in the 'schedule' as well. I just remembered that the poet George Drosinis from Messologi has also written a very beautiful poem about the myth of Aneliagos:

To the prince of Trikardo, that lonesome child

The fates had cast a curse upon

Once the sun would shine this prince forlorn

Instantly, he would have died

And the king father, hoping to save his son

From the sun's evil and burning eye

Built deep, and had the dark defy

A palace in the earth we walk upon.

Years went by... The old man perished

And cometh the time to reign

For handsome Prince, to remain

As the sole Lord of Trikardo to be cherished

And King Aneliagos spends his days

Deep in his palace and only at night

When dark, no light in sight

Hills he roams and champaigns.
And fair Lady Rini saw him one night
In the castle yard, hunting, the sky was lit
And love sparked in her heart's pit
And blazed, for the man in the moon's light...
And now King Aneliagos, like every noble King
His kingdom leaves behind, all night long
Lying in her bed, lulled by her song.
In his happiness though, his fate he does not forget
And before the crack of dawn, before the daystar arose
He leaves in bed alone the fairest rose
And heads to his castle until again, the sun is set.
Lady Rini questions him anew, but to no avail
Why before daybreak he departs! He does not reply
And dark the grasp of jealousy, her heart to ply
And grabs firmly Lady Rini, it does not fail
Such is the hold that makes the cunning Lady to devise
And slay all roosters in the castle, once and for all
So the handsome man in deep sleep will fall
And the sun near the hills and soon to arise.
King Aneliagos is fooled at dawn!
And before he reaches Trikardo, close to old Mani[9].
Alas, the sun was weeping, tears of golden honey
died the King, as a defenceless pawn.
You were right about the myth of Aneliagos. It is a myth that really makes you think."

"You remember that I had analysed it before I narrated it."

"Yes, darling, I could see that you were thinking about something. I remember you saying before that the height is torturing the truth and that the height dies forever in the depth of the light!"

"And later on it turns into a myth, whose roots we have to find."

"So there is some kind of a core in the myth?"

"Of course! It doesn't matter if it is a myth, as Thoukidides tells us in his second book, paragraph 102."

"Do you remember the name of the village, Constantine?"

"Yes! It says exactly this in translation: "They say that Alcmaeon[10] son of Amphiaraus was wandering after the murder of his mother, because all the earth was polluted by his crime. Alcmaeon, as they say, didn't realise that and as he noticed the banks of the river Achelous, he thought that he could settle in the area in order to survive, because since he had killed his mother he had been wandering for a really long time. After he settled at Oiniades, he became a king and gave the new name of the area meaning 'child of Akarnana'. This is what we learnt about Alcmaeon.."

"I can see some connection." said Helen.

"This is where I think that the connection with the myth comes from. It is clear that this city slowly became depopulated and its history was covered by the dust of time. The tradition, obviously, kept only the core. The crime of Alcmaeon, as every crime, is a sequence of the darkness that is spreading, even though that the necklace and the veil of harmony[11] that were presented to his mother Erifilly[12] brought with them everything else, but harmony! And so, they still become a 'mean' for the blur of the pragmatic psychological harmony. The land was never sunny and there was no earth when he killed his mother. In new lands, in new domes, the light is bright and uncovers the regrets that the water of oblivion of the soul is hiding in it. Exactly as it was during the last years the area of the Oiniades. Then you tremble and you writhe. Then the light kills death and from it grows another life. Maybe Oedipus got blinded by the light of the truth so that he cannot see his… regrets?"

"But really, what is that makes people to collapse and writhe in the light?"

"The glow of truth is burning, my love!"

"True! The glow of truth is burning."

"And this I think is the light from the myth. Because everything is hiding something. The myth is born in reality and always carries the reality. The sunflowers are changing their shape. The light of thought, the patience and the endurance show the sunward faces in the heavy winter."

"Darling, your thoughts' sharp pickaxe makes holes in the infertile soil. Then you find the glow in the words. Then the sun starts shining in your pickaxe! But please, sit for a while. Come close to me, into my arms."

"We have to sit for a while especially now when the spring waters are pushing you into one unstoppable line, we have to hold our hands tightly! Where do you reckon that this line stops? How does the recreation of the run stop, the merge with the joy, the soulmate of Solomon? When does the bullet of the thought explode? Maybe where the straight line ends?"

"Nowhere, love! Altogether they die slowly sucked by the dry life and all that is left is a rotten leaf."

"My dear, it becomes food for something else that will return to life at some point. Everything lives and everything dies from life!"

"Which one of those two did we accept, Constantine?"

"Your question, my love, gave me the answer..."

"Because you believe the same as well. We are not going to die because of life. we are going to live because of life!"

"Constantine, I dreamt about a sea with a dawn that is bathing in its calm waters…"

"I saw it in your eyes by the rays of the dawn. And your hair is a ladder for me to climb to the stars, up there, far away, in your shining face. To bend at the calm waters of your soul and to drink your sweetness and to listen to the whisper of your heart and your breath!"

"I dreamt about a garden with fragrant flowers. I found them in your soul!"

"What would you need the lonely garden for if the petals of your lips are not its accessories, a cooling rose, from whose aroma I can get drunk?"

"While the weather tries to destroy it and the North winds are blowing, it always stands with its soul in his hands."

"And so life never dies!"

"I enfolded you in my own world and I am holding you so that we can go. Let's go where the dawn caresses the living and signs the graves of the death."

"Let's go to the rough paths of the rocks. We seeded our words in the bowels of the valley. I missed the land because it's you that makes it beautiful. Pay attention to the rocks, only to the rocks!"

"We are going to climb the rocks, Constantine, the pebbles will squeak. This is where I first saw the dawn. It was in April."

"You said it. So all the joy comes from April. Maybe you saw the joy to fly on its green branches and it stayed during April and it was sharing it with you?"

"When joy is a gift you have to be afraid of it. What would you give in exchange? If you give the same gift, then you didn't need it. And so, it was not joy! If you give something else, you will get disappointed when you see it thrown away."

"Then what is joy?"

"The same as truth! One unknown X!"

"In reality the real numbers give a value to X."

"It's as we say, Constantine: "Not everything that shines is gold"."

"And I want to add "We test the gold in fire". And then, from this test, from this torture, we can prove if it is real gold or… fake!"

I don't know why we were conversing for such a long time on these topics. Maybe it was the satisfaction that we had found its value - the unknown X. It was called 'joy'. It was something that we were looking for years in muddy waters, black and white boards. We had forgotten only ourselves. And here we found her and we both shouted together: "Here she is! Joy!"

Her words were like the water from the spring. Clearer than gold. And her voice was sweeter than the one of the nightingale that cheeps on the branches of the trees full with newborn leaves. We reached the rocks. As if they were sweating from the battle for the night! As if it was cold sweat on a face that is full of fear. Helen was looking at them with awe... I was looking at the bank. The sunbeams were showing up slowly on the horizon…

---

1 Lady-Rini. *Daughter of the emperor Alexis Palaiologou, wife of the emperor Adronikos, famous for the eponym palace at the place of Ancient Plevrona, that is located in the flounces of Arakynth, Northwest from Messologi. For the people Lady-Rini was famous for her love for the king Aneliagos (look also number 2).*

2 Aneliagos. *Prince, the only son of king Trikardo, at the place of the old city of Oiniades, that is located in the homonym hill "Trikardo" close to the outfalls of the river Achelous and 4 kilometres west from the modern village Katohi in Akarnania. The mythical creator of the city of Oiniades was the murderer of his own mother Alchmaeon, who was guided to the area by a prophecy of the Delphic oracle (look also Alchmaeon in the same chapter).*

3 Oiniades. *Look at "Aneliagos" above.*

4 Katohi. *Look at "Aneliagos" above.*

5 Trikardo. *Look at "Aneliagos" above.*

6 "You defeated me, Nazareth". *It's a phrase that the emperor of Byzantium Julian "The Apostat" (361 to 363) pronounced just before he died. He was the one that in 362 restores the national religion, establishing the beginning of independent religion. The closed ancient temples were open and the church property was given back to its owners. The Christians were removed from the high political and military services, and were banned from being teachers in the schools of the Empire. On 26 June 363 he was wounded by a spear in the liver during fights with scattered Persian forces. Julian then died with the words "You defeated me, Nazareth, recognising the futility of his effort to revive the ancient* *religion. However, the phrase is disputed historically.*

7 Asfaka. *A bush that is found usually in brushwoods and rocky hills, usually on top of limestone suppositories, from low to middle heights, very favourite of the bees because of the juice of its flowers.*

8 Plevron. *An ancient city that is located on the hill Gyftokastro and Petrovouni, 1.5 kilometres Northwest from the Messologi and the county Aetilokarnania. Look also "Lady-Rini" and "Aneliagos".*

9 Palaio-Mani. *The modern village Palaiomanina, which is built on the top of one endless ancient city on the west bank of the river Achelous.*

10 Alcmaeon or Alcmaion. *Hero of the ancient Greek mythology, the son of Amphiaraos Eriphyle, who was bribed by Polynices with the offer of the necklace of Cadmus wife Harmony. Spurred by an oracle decided to avenge his father and killed his mother, aided by his brother Amphilocus. After his matricide he was hunted by the Erynies. The rest is mentioned in the text.*

11 Harmony. *See above "Alcmaeon."*

12 Eriphyle. *See above "Alcmaeon."*

CHAPTER FOUR

Memories: Death is preparing
for a hit at the rocks

And even if death is scattering at such hours, where will the roots of youth go to drink the last drop that was left from the fire of the sun? No, death would not be able to take away from me her laughter, her soul, her dream. I had her blossoms before March and then in April I sat to drink the water from her buds. And even though the dawn hereafter didn't find the buds, it recognised them in their cracking when they were opening their petals to praise life.

But everything is the same, as it seemed, as I saw them. They were alive because life in their hands had turned into a game. And they live with the water of the moments that is not vinegar. I can see them all next to you are old, older and they all become younger, because they are protected in the endless sea of memories. They are alive, they run in front of it, they are calling you, they are shouting:

"The rocks! The rocks!"

"Darling, because of them I moved, even then. How do you want me to forget the grave of the beautiful? Ah, how hard are the hits of time. Without time to take a breath, you run in the muddy waters and when you hit the land, the thorns are drowning you! How could I deny the land that presented me with its springs so that I can drink the water all the time, so that I could quench my thirst on the crossroads of life? We are Oedipus![1]. And now when I am sitting in their shadow, one path is forcing me to go to the rocks. Life has crouched in one lens of thoughts and illuminates. It doesn't bring you back so many years. It always pushes you further not at well known paths, but at the same idols, the same words, words that you believe in. You keep on going and you are looking for the same. So it didn't die! How could something innocent die? Which force breaks the barrier of faith in one idea? Back then the same shore was pushing me to its path. The voice was the same as the one from today. Of course, my steps on the pavement were not accompanied by hers. I can still hear her words though, I see her face, her image, her joy. It is horrible to live with her absence, to be drowning in memories and to hear the voice from the shore. And this cottage that is covering my own bowels I hadn't seen since then. I couldn't dig my thoughts straight away. I wouldn't be able to recognise the light so quickly. But the voices, the same voices were telling me the same: to keep on going.

I had to keep walking, because only this means strength!

I had to keep walking, because only this means strength!

Just like before, I wanted to see her, to cool down my soul from the burning rays of life, to stand in her garden, my garden, she will greet me, she will kiss me with her sweet mouth and bathe me with the light of her eternal smile.

Now I can hear her words, her poems, her clear thoughts, the gargle of the springs of the valley. The world is melting in my palms and we are leaving it to melt us in its fire. Where are we going to live? Where do our eyes get cloudy from the spin of our existence, where does the sky of our lives becomes all chaotic and we start counting storms. Because we put the spears of hatred as borders and we close ourselves in walls of bodies. The land of the rocks showed it. And I connected it with the labyrinth of my head. When I came out, I saw light! But how many hits needs someone so that they stop being a body? How many times must one confront life to forget that they are dying? How many graves- food for the worms –must one see to understand that the cheap life can be measured with a metre of earth? People, leave the bands of power free for yourself, for the people, for the world. What would you gain if you mix up your thoughts with the other people's business?

Enough, I left my thoughts away from my idol. I don't go anymore to the rocks, where the light feathers of memory brought her to show me the same, the eternal path that I walk down back then as well. And back then we found ourselves at the rocks at the time of sunrise and she told me:

"Only one sunset is able to bring in its red hair this image of the sunrise!"

"My love, I swear in your image that the sunrises are going to remind us of the sunsets!…"

"Darling, I swear that you have the dawn in front of you! The sunsets open the dark chambers with the preserved vows!…"

"Helen, if one could lose the rocks from one's eyes, when they are close to them, then I will spread my oaths in the valley of oblivion!"

"No, Constantine! You wouldn't be able to close your ears to the sough of the leaves of the forest of your soul."

"I don't need Delphic tripods for prophecies. We are the ones that erect Pythia[2] in front of us and she is stopping us with her smoke to choose the way that is only one inbetween many others, covered with nettle…"

"Darling, do you think that there are no other forces that interract with the people's deeds along their way?"

"Yes, but not different from the 'invisible' human forces. The human himself, I repeat, is responsible for his own deeds. All the rest is a cheap excuse."

"Therefore the rocks are not responsible for their height or their pebbles!…"

"Ah! Why are you mixing up with people something that people are abusing! The rocks and every height are a symbol of death, as well as the cross and the marble stone on top of the grave. That doesn't mean though that they are responsible for death. And so, we are torturing ourselves, because there is no real value, the truth is not shining!"

"Constantine, the values and the truth, they are shining even without them!"

"The rocks, darling, they make it shinier, or even better: the rocks make us notice the light even more."

"Because they are… torturing it!"

"Helen, I just remembered what my father used to say about the rocks. I didn't pay any attention to it before. Now, in the middle of the vapours of reality I find your reasons."

"And so the rocks are death!…"

"Exactly. The rocks are their death! The rocks become flat and at their place comes the real value, the real ideas, the real love, the 'good and beautiful' person, that has escaped his fate and became its charioteer!"

"Constantine, Golgotha and the Caucasian rocks would not die if at them love to humanity was not tortured. Only it remained at its place, it took roots and covered the world of our soul. Even though he got vinegar instead of water, is this the only poison that the frog-people can offer? He became a breath that blew at the dried from the hot wind of hatred hearts."

"And these rocks have become the symbol of hatred. In the middle, where the ravine is, they had become the thrones of the powerful ones. The first sunbeams were finding the 'caretakers' on their throne. The others were kneeling, worshipping the foreign soil so that at the end they could take a bit of crops. A bit of soil was not enough for their rocky hands. Ironically, the dust was covering their faces, so that they can never see the colours of the day. From there the signal of the midday rest was given- just as long as they can eat something- and of the afternoon work until sunset. The working hours that the powerful ones have imposed was for the weak ones 'from sun to sun', and so with the sun they were starting working in the villages and with the end of the sun, ended work as well!"

She stopped. She glanced at the heights above her and then she looked at me, I couldn't imagine so much…'usefulness'. But why the 'history' of the rocks would make me so hostile and I wouldn't narrate the historical reality?

"Skull location, Helen. There are always 'skull locations', made by bones and one prophet in the middle of them shouting 'naked bones'. The truth is naked in front of us. Are we the prophets or are we turning the others into prophets? Why are we afraid of the truth? "Son of human, say your prophecy!" Stand in the middle and shout. Stones will fall into your feet and they will close the road. And later on "regrets at the ruins"."

"But we were not made of stone dust and indestructible calcium. We were made from mud, so that we can hold the stones together, putting them in the foundations, in the walls."

"So that later on they soak in the tears of destruction, of misery and failure!"

"Constantine, there are voices more real and more true, more clear and more loud than our own. At the end, our voices become one with denial that is called regret. You don't need the candle for all that! On that narrow path where the human falls slowly, walks in circles, runs to the exit, but it becomes more and more narrow. And the head becomes older. The proof for that is the 'execution' of Jesus. The human buries the previous people and if he finds a new one, we have to find his grave empty with one voice of white soul saying "he's not here anymore". The sign of the old person and the 'types of exhaustion'. This is the seal of the trial. The 'execution' is the beginning of the new."

"And what about the higher ones, Helen?" I asked.

"The atrocious martyr who sees the dead - ghosts that step on him and he screams: 'Light, water, Life!'"

"Darling, the stones have started to burn from the sun, after they have sucked even the last drop of the night."

"It's the sun that burns them. The top is on fire. The heart is in flames. The soul sparkles from hatred. Where are the shadows of the plane trees of love that take in their hug the 'flock'? Look, the bushes in the reeds. Soon the sheep will come. It will cool down in their shadowy palm. What can you do about the points of the rocks? The sheep were rushing down quickly with their heads bent towards the earth, leaving behind them a cloud of dust. Bells, whistles and barking were accompanying the dust cloud."

"Constantine, the one that is coming towards us, isn't that Mitros?"

"Yes, one mosquito without worries!"

"Well, let's use some mosquito repellent then!" she said laughing.

Mitros greeted us from afar, waving with the crook. He had his jacket pitched on one of his shoulders and from the other was hanging his bag. He was coming closer.

"Hello, kids. How are you, Constantine? Miss Helen we see every now and then. But you, Constantine, where have you been?"

"Welcome, Mitros, what news do you bring to us from the valley?"

"Nothing, Constantine. We, as you can see, don't do anything except from taking care of the sheep. This is our job."

"You are right. But you could say something about your job." I added.

"Outdoor work and stories of beasts, nights with full moon and spring days, it's always the same. I've told the stories to Helen in her home when she was little."

"I remember, Mitros. They are interesting the stories of outdoor work."

"They are interesting to listen to, but not as much to live."

"Well, that's your job, as you already said." I said.

"Ok then. You tell me something about the Capital. They told me you came the day before yesterday. As soon as you came, you didn't stay at all at the village. That's what they told me! The wildness is attracting you as a magnet. That's what they said!"

"I can see, Mitros, that you know a lot of things apart from your job." I noticed.

"What can we do, Constantine? If we don't talk about something, time stops! Without wanting, you start talking to the others and then we talk about the others' news!"

"So the proverb is true when it says that 'The poor and the peasant worry about other people's concerns.'!"

"It's good this proverb that you just said. It's true. And now I can tell you something else that's new."

"Let's hear it then." said Helen.

"It's connected to Helen as well. And to you, Constantine, so and so!"

"Oh come on, don't make us worry about it."

"Helen, I just saw your sister Alexandra on her way to the house."

"Where, in the cottage?"

"Yes! Your uncle George was taking her."

"She had told me that she will be coming the day before August 15th. It looks like she got bored in the village of my uncle."

"Liakos told me that Alexandra heard about Constantine's arrival and this is why she came over earlier! Well, she wants some company. I think that she was jealous! I am sorry for talking like this, but it is because I love you two!…"

"Thank you, Mitros, for your good news."

"Not such good news, Helen. She is going to ruin your plans!"

"What plans, Mitros?" asked Helen, somewhat puzzled.

"I am going to tell you a story. My father who passed used to tell me this story always, as if he wanted to uncover something I had always hidden in my heart. He used to tell me: All these things are dust in the eyes..."

Helen was laughing. I was looking at the tanned face of the shepherd and from his eyelids was hanging the dirty skin of slyness. He gave us few glances so that he can study our reactions better and after he drank some water from his flask, he went on talking.

"You see, for many years now, Thanasis Loggos, Nicola's father, who was famous for stealing goats, once went to Panos Liontas to bring him one stolen goat to slaughter it and to sell it, because he was the butcher of the village. Panos told him that as soon as he sells the goat, he will pay him off. The goat was slaughtered and sold, but Panos didn't give the money. Thanasis escaped, because he couldn't even tell to the people in the village that Panos didn't give him the money, because the goat was stolen! You see, it was stolen! He was thinking, thinking and then he found a solution. In summer Panos was sleeping in the garden and Thanasis knew that. How could he take his sack though, as he was always keeping it under his pillow? He filled his bag with dust, slowly came near Panos and threw all the dust in his eyes. Before Panos could realise what was happening, Thanasis took the bag and disappeared. This is how Thanasis took Panos' bag. But he made a mistake, because there was not even a broken penny inside!"

We laughed. We understood the slyness of Mitros and Helen asked:

"So, in whose face did we throw dust and for what reason, Mitros?"

"Ah, you naughty children, naughty! You want to make fun of me. But it's ok, kids, you are young, you want to have fun…"

"What is all this that you are saying, Mitros," I asked,"Are you going mad?"

"I am alright; the world has gone crazy..."

"And you with it…" I said.

"And me… sneaky buddy," he replied with a laugh so ugly that was even worse than the foxiness hidden in the niches of his eyes…

"It doesn't matter, Mitros. Thank you."

"See you at the feast the day after tomorrow then."

"Look, Mitros, I almost forgot. Please don't forget the lamb for the day after tomorrow," said quickly Helen.

"I will bring it for your father Vassilis. I will bring him the best and the biggest lamb! I am leaving you now, goodbye!"

"Good luck, Mitros."

He was walking quickly. His head was bent as if thousands of sly thoughts were making it heavier. In a bit he disappeared from our eyes. Helen sat next to me, put her hand around my shoulders and started thinking.

"What are you thinking about, dear?"

"I can still hear the 'mosquito words'!"

"Didn't I tell you that the 'mosquito' is coming?"

"Why do we care though?" said Helen.

"We don't care about the mosquito of course! But its poison… Let's forget about this." I added.

"Let's keep this in mind. Mitros is a very, very bad person," I said, reminding what I had just 'predicted'.

"Oh yes, Constantine! I am afraid of people."

"You don't need to be afraid of them as much as you need to look in front of yourself and to be safe," I said and I kissed her lips smelling of petals.

"That's true, dear. But let's go under the shadow down there, close to the spring. today it's going to be very hot."

We got up. I took her hand and we started walking. She looked very thoughtful. The heat was fluttering everywhere and the shadow was pulling us by the feet. We reached. The waters were in a hurry, they greeted us, as they were moving in the small trenches. The green grass did not bend its heads. It didn't hide bad thoughts! It was alive and they was spreading life everywhere. In the deep shadow we found relief and on the green carpetrest. We sat down.

What do you want! Everything knees, bends and warps when the wind blows. This doesn't show death! It drags death and puts it on a pedestal. We have to be careful of its strength. Love is an oasis in the desert! Endurance is a green tuft in the summer heat. Why would you want to dig it out with the spear of hatred? You should water it with as much clean water as life can give you. Where are you going to find, you poor hiker, the strength to keep walking? The dried thorns are strangling you, you burn together with them and you turn into a carbon when the sun hits you.

The sheep are all huddling under the shadow, the shepherds are gone to their homes and a bell breaks the silence. Everything has given into the hugs of time and peace. Time has stopped. Humans are its helpers. What would he be measuring with his steps in the reeds? Now you can hear better his steps. In his croups the denial is spreading all the question marks and all that is left is one NO. I could not stand the silence. But who said such thing. She talked. How could the stalks of my soul shake from the wind without winter? But she was looking at the clear sky, the damp calmness of her soul. I was sure! I made the foundation of the idol with human materials, I supported it with the power of my soul and I covered it with the clear thought of 'so that'. It's all the same. And the voice is the same, mixed with one more, always new:

"The rocks! The rocks!"

I had to keep walking, because only this means strength.

"Darling, your thoughts run without a brake…"

"They are, dear, together with yours, at the rocks with the carnivores eagles!…All my thoughts are next to you, my sweet thought. They are all standing with their bodies from heaven, trying to forget your image. But I could never forget your voice."

"Let's go, Constantine, to the rocks, to the lakes, to the daffodils."

At that time they were bright green and were spread all over the valley. Now they are all dry. You, my love, in my thoughts you are always in front of me and you reject the abrasive hours of life. Next to me, in front of me, with me. I never denied your land. It was mine as well. I hear your voice in your poems that I have in front of me, just like then at the springs. I can hear you, just like then. Your melodic voice is accompanying me always. It's always with my eyes, my thought, my Life...

———————

1 Oedipus. *The most tragic person in the Ancient Greek mythology. He was son of the king of Thebes Laius and Jocasta. Before Oedipus' birth, the king of Thebes Laius wanted to learn what his fate was in connection to the fact that his wife was not able to get pregnant until then. Apollo through Pythia, informed him that he will have son, but the son is going to kill him. At the end, the prophecy became true. Oedipus killed his father, who was on his way to Pythia, became the king of Thebes and married... his mother Jocasta! He had four children from Jocasta: Polynices, Eteocles, Antigone and Ismene, who were his siblings at the same time. This is how the prophecy that Pythia gave first to Laius and then to Oedipus became true. After the truth came out, Oedipus blinded himself and Jocasta hung herself...*

2 Pythia. *This is how every High Priestess in the temple of Apollo in Delphi was called. She was transferring the prophecies to the visitors while in a ecstatic state in a way usually short, hard to understand and enigmatic.*

CHAPTER FIVE

Memories: Fulfilling of love at the Spring

Spontaneously and strongly I took her velvet-like left hand in mine. We started walking towards the rocks, the mountain fountain. The ravine was constantly lighted by the sun, while the rocks were accompanying our happy steps with their gigantic wild eyes. The distance from our last stop was not so big, where our love reached a culmination and constantly was pushing us to get in contact flesh to flesh.

We reached the pit with the spring. You would think that its fountain opened our hands so that it can cool down our faces with even more gargling water. Around it bright green bushes and weeds, but also wild flowers were trying to survive the heat of August, as if they had prepared a green bed, so that we can taste our love after the hymn of love at our previous stop.

"How beautiful you are, my love! How beautiful are your eyes! Come, close to me, very close to me, so that we can hug each other tightly and dissolve the hymn of passion in our bodies! What to see and what to caress for the first time? Your eyes with intense lines under the rich eyelashes? Your rose cheeks? Your lips like red lace? Your sweet voice? Your white neck covered with the curls of your golden hair? Your wonderful breast, "Thy two breasts are like two young roes that are twins", like Solomon says?"

"My love, all these are sheep in the wild flowers of my soul when the sunrise comes and the darkness is gone!"

"You are so beautiful, darling! Nothing on you is needless. You conquered my heart , just like in 'Song of the Songs'!"

"Come next to me, let's lay down on the grass next to the spring so that we can celebrate our life. Soul mate. My love."

"Come, my love. Kiss me, kiss me."

"Your lips, my love, they are dripping honey, honey and you hold milk under your tongue."

"Let me caress your large breasts like wheels in a wet garden with pomegranates."

"I was waiting for you for two years at a calm spring. I was going to sleep, but my heart was awake. And now I didn't hear only the knock of my beloved one on the door, but also these hands to hold me tight with joy that fills my whole soul."

"Open your arms, my soul mate, let me caress you with my breasts! Throw your clothes in the grass to decorate the wild flowers!"

"Now when love came and is right next to me, I will lay down straight away to feel the chills in the depth of my insights. It is my beloved one, with eyes of a wild dove, with lips like red lotus, wet and aromatic. Your mouth is lustful, all of it is pleasure. You are mine."

"I will continue the hymn to the loved one that you started and our love will be fulfilled:

"Come to me, my love, to the endless meadows,

on the green carpet, where the wild flowers blossom.

We will roll there all night long and like a sprig of lilac

Our love will blossom

in the centre of the fire circle of the poppies"."

We were looking at the August moon, hugging, with extreme joy, with our nude bodies writhing on the calm grass, there at the waterfall.

"I was keeping the seed of pleasure, darling, clean and unpolluted, just for you…"

"…And I was keeping my valley of pleasure and fertility just for you and I was saving it for you to spread your seed and so the bud of my soul can grow…"

"…And now I tidy with the hands of my soul your valley of pleasure…"

"…And I, a garden all blossomed and fragrant, give myself into you…"

"Eternal idol, made by thoughts instead of cornerstones, decorated with vapours of a dream, I am next to you, but you are always next to me. In front of me always, since you mix with the threads of my thoughts and the urges of my love. I can see you in these leaves that you spreaded for all those that wanted from their close ones to see life."

"Constantine, I can see in front of me Mitros smiling all the time. His eyes throw flames, he is coming nearer, but his flames can never burn us."

"How is it possible, especially with the fulfilment of our love, one cloud made of winter to make even the spring sky ugly? It is winter, winter. we have to recognise its joy! There it is, one smile!"

"Next to you I found sun rays in the winter cold" she said, pressing her lips against mine. "Can I tell you few poems of mine?"

"The poems in these hours are like a white dove that was left in the unquenchable thirst of the Wandering Rocks[1]. After that comes our ship."

"Constantine, I am going to read them to you, I am going to read them to you, even if the August sun burns even more the grass around us!

In the wild weather an offspring
is silence.
In the winter a sunbeam
is hope.
In the heaviness of night
a counterweight -
endurance.
In slow steps of oblivion -
the rush of the thoughts.
In the waves of the sea steady peddals
the desire,

on the path of thorns for a cleaner
faith
was
when
in the turns of time
I didn't lose myself."

"How could you, darling, lose yourself in the turns of time, when it is turning to escape from your dazzling rhythm? One molecule that jumped from its chariot in the ravine with the daffodils!"

"Yes, dear, how all comes out at the ravine, the weeds are suffocating and the rocks burn the iron of malice so that they can invade even more sharply in the eyes!"

"It is something even worse than the story of the dust in the eyes that Mitros told us. Its smile is a hole of an oven!"

"And about the Wandering Rocks? Let me hear."

"Listen to my poem:
Argo,
We passed the Wandering Rocks
with the help from the white dove.
In the mania of the crush
the rocks melted and on the way back
offended wreaked
in the shatter of hate.

Can I go on?"

"Of course!"

"This one is yours, ours! Listen to it:
Argo,

open the sails to go to new Colchis.

Steersman I will be, as help from Aeolus[2] we'll have

the trident of Poseidon[3]

we will break the will of the rocks.

Pelion is waiting for us

to meet the peace in the Aegeon

the happiness"

"Thank you, Constantine! But how many Wandering Rocks does one need to pass before reaching Colchis?"

"As long as Mitros exists! They are trying to shoot with the rocks from their hearts every white dove."

"Enslaved hands for slaves, carved by slave hands… How can fake Delphic tripods not crumble when they hear these words? How can you not fence your garden from soul stealing deaths that are chasing you? That's why the vultures have filled the sky and down there they line up the carcasses with no flesh that they don't need."

"And you, my flame, were talking about dark roads. But I am holding the flame together with me, because we turn it on together. You held it up in your hands and you are giving light to everyone! I knew that you were waiting for my arrival! You told me and you read for me. I am listening to you. I am always listening to you, just like that time at the bank of the river, just like now in your temple, in your notebook sown with a fertile seed to give birth to life. And it did, even though back then I was seeding the seed of love in your heart:

Calm fountain in your feet,

in your cold watery lips,

shadows of plane trees in your mouth,

shield for the fire

arrows of Apollo[4]

Fragrant flowers in your garden

blossoming and I wait

like Persephone[5] the chariot of spring

Flower-drinking bee

the flower-milk to drink."

"Constantine, are you going to continue looking at the sky, your hymn, your own hymn of love?"

"Not, darling, staring at the fake sky, but at your own sky, in your eyes, in your beauty, in your lips, in your breasts, in your body, in your eyes, your hair, your small feet…"

"Dear, I did not expect after the culmination of the hymn to love, such Solomonian words!"

"My love, down there at the bottom of the hill, we created our hug and we destroyed the world, we sprayed it with the drops from our eyes of youth and in the water we threw its dying roots. But something remained in the land of the shadows. There remained the moving shadows, that are made only to follow us, when the light is falling straight into their eyes and in their Centaurian faces!"

---

1 The Wandering Rocks. *In Greek mythology, they looked like two big rocks at the sides of a sea channel, that were coming together and separating all the time, so that they made the safe sailing in-between them impossible. The first ship that ever succeeded to pass them was the ship Argo with the Argonauts, with the help of Goddess Hera and the advice of Phineas to let first a white dove to pass between them, and it worked. The rocks closed behind the dove and it lost only few feathers of its tail, and when they reopened, Argo passed with the Argonauts paddling with all their strength. Since then the two rocks stopped moving.*

2 Aeolus. *In Greek mythology, he was chosen by Zeus as the keeper of the winds. He was holding them in his bag and was letting them out by order of Zeus.*

3 Poseidon. *In Greek mythology he is the God of the land and the sea, of the rivers, fountains and drinkable water.*

4 Apollo. *In Greek mythology he was a very important good with around 350 pseudonyms,* *functions and local cults, a healer, a clairvoyant, and also God of the sun ("Phoebus"), and also the God with the silver arrows. In Odysseus Homer mentions that Apollo's lyre and Apollo's bow are the same thing. The bow that injures hits in the chest and it kills and it also brings the same harmony with the lyre, when Apollo takes it in his hands, Demodicus and Phemius. The bow of Apollo as a killing organ is represented in the verses of Odysseus about the murder of the candidate fiancés by Odysseus. As soon as Odysseus continued his long and successful rule, his priority became the order and the happiness of creation. The name of the bow is "bios" and "bios" means life, and it's act is death... used to say Heraclitus.*

5 Persephone. *Daughter of the Goddess Demeter. Her father was Zeus and her husband was Hades. Hades took her to the Underworld because of her beauty. However, Demeter asked for him to bring her back. Hades agreed that Persephone would come back for six months and then go back to the Underworld for the next six months. This is why when she is up, Demeter is happy and then there is good weather, while for the rest six months the weather was bad.*

CHAPTER SIX

Memories: Strange visits
at the rocks with omens

It is still midday. Time seals its walks. It becomes smaller at the corner of its turn and turns into a small grain! So, let's cool it now while it is still warm.

"Constantine, I hear a voice. John is coming."

"John. Which John?"

"John Costoulas!"

"I love the world, Constantine;" Helen said to me, somehow scared. "In your face I start loving the world, the human, even if he is food for the worms, even if he is swamp for the mosquitoes."

"This is exactly why I started loving him. Because I figured him out! Truth is hidden in the shell of a lie, just like the almond in its wooden pod. Break it and you will find it. Break the fences and you will be able to smell the aromatic flowers of the garden."

"Hello to you, kids. Hello, my friends, Helen and Constantine…"

"Hi, John. Which good wind brought you to the valley?"

"The… sirocco!"

"Don't forget that the sirocco is just passing by," I replied."But whoever finds it on their way, burns down!"

"Sit down, John, so that we can see you." said Helen.

"I am dripping from sweat."

"Be careful, because sweat freezes at cold surfaces."

"Alright, Constantine. I will be careful. Just you don't freeze me more…"

"John, my friend, we will offer you our hugs, our company and I admit that I cannot find words to thank you for coming to keep us company." I said.

"Thank you for your nice words and I am sorry for your bad deeds!"

"But they are... good."

"Yes, but you didn't make me cry..."

"So you accept them..."

"No, I'm just standing them..."

"Then you are strong."

"What are you, guys, saying, so laconically," said Helen.

"I, Helen, am giving an oral exam. These are the answers I can give. This is as much as I have read!"

"Come, John, sit next to me and let's talk about the old times."

"If my friend Constantine lets me."

"I am not used to giving orders to free and intelligent people. Because you are used to give orders though and to take orders, I... permit you, with Helen's approval of course, of course!"

"You passed through the village as a thunder and you went straight to Vassilis Skrakos."

"And where was I supposed to go, John? I don't have anyone in the village. As you know, my parents' house is empty. Everyone, my father and my brothers have left for Germany and Athens..."

"You could have come to my house! Or may be you don't want to come anymore, because you took your diploma? You are forgetting that once, when we were going together to secondary school, I was buying you, my father was buying you, all the books from fifth grade, because you were poor!"

"The books cannot be repaid with one visit, John…"

"I am sorry, Constantine, I didn't believe that it would bother you…"

"No, please. I was afraid that you were bothered by it…"

"Water and salt, Constantine, leave all these," interrupted Helen.

"This reminds me of 'earth and water'!![1]. But let's talk about something else…"

"Does that have something to do with me, Constantine?"

"But, you didn't ask us anything like this, even though you are… on fire!"

"Hm… How can you sit here in the valley?"

"The fumes don't reach here." I said.

"You wouldn't say that there are fumes in the village." he argued.

"Maybe it reminds you of… fumes"

"The village is preparing for the festival of Virgin Mary on the 15th of August. The festival on the 15th of August. Do you remember with how much joy we were expecting it?"

"We were children too. Back then we were waiting for them to water us with joy." I said. "Today the whole world is about the… feast." I added.

"And the madness about the… rocks," he said, throwing the glove.

"The rocks are yours and you can get rid of the… madness." I said.

"Ok, Constantine, you made me laugh…"

"What do you need, John. You have properties, you have sheep and shepherds…"

"What to do with all these, Constantine! What to do with them when you are suffocating from the fumes of the soul… as you hinted."

"Aren't you ashamed, you big landowner's child, to talk like this?" said

Helen.

"I had to study as well. Now I am hitting my head. I didn't listen to you. I envy you, Constantine. I am jealous of you, Helen…"

"Education is just weeding on the human soul. But your soul, John, is not hoeing. Neither do the rocks. The rocks crush down." I said allegorically.

"I took the road for the rocks, as if one giant force was pushing me and was giving wings to my feet, was stirring my brain, was splashing my face like a run on a muddy road and I could not stop myself."

"You are saying too much, John," I said "Don't think that we don't understand you…"

Helen caressed John's face, she saw his passion, but what could she do about it? What does an innocent person can do for a guilty one? What could she give him to pall his passion? Love is something completely different. You don't create passion, so that you can find love. However, love doesn't grow in the rocky mountains! Love shines at the rocks! And it is higher than them. It's in the dome of the soul, in its sky.

He couldn't even look up with his dark eyes. He couldn't even speak. He couldn't even hold himself. Is it possible not to feel the flames of love? Helen was cutting off the buds of lust and of his passion with her own power, but at its place grew fire tongues. I couldn't give anything from my own love. I was a good friend of him, but in this case, my image was sinking in my full with hatred eyes.

"When are you leaving, Constantine?" John asked uncomfortably.

"In the evening, John." I said. "We will go to find some coolness. Sit down, we are going to have some nice time…"

"I am leaving. I have some work in the village."

"As you wish." I said.

"You can come tomorrow morning if you want though. We will wait for you at the rocks. We will climb to the top, we will sing and we will leave as soon as Mitros comes with the lamb." interrupted Helen.

"Yes, John, don't refuse to share the joy of your two friends from childhood."

"Alright. Tomorrow morning I will meet you at the rocks." he replied, somehow thoughtfully, scratching his head. If it is only for Mitros' lamb, there is no need for you to come as well, Helen…"

"No, I just want the three of us to be together." said Helen honestly. "But don't come moody like you are now."

"Ok, I am leaving now." he said with his head bent.

"It is very, very hot, my friend." I noticed.

"I will walk to the village slowly-slowly. Goodbye now." he said, looking serpent-like as he was walking away…

"Good luck, John, and as we arranged." said Helen.

He took the shortcut at the canes with a walk that looked like Mitros' walk! So strange! He didn't even look back. The same force that was pushing him on his way to here, was pushing him away to somewhere else, but where I asked myself. Helen was staring somewhere far, as if she was trying to put the brakes on something that wanted to go on a route to somewhere, the route to the steep descent! And while you are watching it move further, disappears in the blur of the eyes and the last breath.

"In the land of the waterfalls, Helen, in the land of the rocks, you can see eagles next to you! Did you see their stinking wings? Did you hear their mean voices? Harpies[2] are emptying our table and in the middle of it they place one word: Death!…"

"Please, Constantine, read your 'Harpies'. I want to hear them. I can see them in front of me!…Let's go forward, Jason…"

"Just a moment, I'm looking for them. They are my old poems… I found them:

The God-sent Harpies

that are feeding on my food,

the fast-winged, nail-crooked virgins,

drive them away, Argonauts.

Hear the hum of them flying to the sky,

Look at the dirt they left.

Olympus got scared and started hating my Light

because I was giving it to others.

Its hills were shaking,

its roots were creaking,

built on the graves of slaves

the fake thrones fell down.

How does Life blur

when they take your Light away,

how the darkness spreads away

and the top marks the sun quickly?

The sound of the Wandering Rocks you can hear,

the violent winds pushing madly the stones.

Black mist in the passage

I didn't it want to dress you.

Let the snow-white dove to fly

and look at the madness"

"There is always one Phineus[3] in a passage, always one Theresias[4] in a dark dale, strength kills with strength. Harpies always tear to pieces the calm eyes that foresee, that tell the future. This is their only problem." said Helen somewhat worried.

"My darling, this is how the world is. All these that wander are not looking for anything else, but food for their hatred. Bended heads like a bird on the ground. But something remains to make the bud blossom, so that life can come out again, stronger and powered by the dirt of the enemies that it stepped on. The strength is always what accompanies the one that wants to live, to die and to resurrect…"

"I was living in a dream my whole life, Constantine. This dream gave birth to an impetuous light that burnt the thorny crown and in its place remained one crown of light."

"I am living this life in the … 'land of the daffodils'. Here we are in the shades. Get ready for the invasion of denial!…'

"I am always with you, close to you, always next to you, my love! Snow white sails are going to inflate and in their wings time will put bow…"

She leaned on me. Where else she could find the genuine prop, leaning on the strong foundations of love? I felt her excitement, I felt her strength in her living breath, in the movement of her firm breasts, "like two young roes that are twins" as the poet says in 'The song of the songs.'. These two young roes that are twins, they are the eternal throne of life, of love!

"Hold me, Constantine, hold me!" she said. "Drive away the Harpies that are surrounding you, that are surrounding us! No, I am not going to let you die, let us die!"

"My love, in the circles of the sun, don't unroll your gore and don't weave the veil of the moon with its thread!"

"No, no" she answered with her sweet voice, "the times are changing, but its centre remains static - Death!"

"Which thoughts, my darling, want to put in the circle that they make around this big circle of life, with its centre that is love? Death hasn't been defeated, even more, the circle of Golgotha was not filled by the garden of Gethsemane."

"Yes, dear! Useless was the arrival of the myrrh bearers. The myrrh bearing thoughts were born from the myrrh bearing solutions! And so they are leaning on death! Otherwise they would not be myrrh bearing…"

"My love, Phineus is cawing! You can hear the banging of the Wandering Rocks. The Harpies are jamming the chaste table of the soul and are trying to establish the eternal light…"

"We are cawing as well, Constantine! The road to love is only one. You have to put to sleep the guardian dragon, 'Hatred, so that you can grab it! Go forward, you people smoked from the fire nostrils of the bulls[5], what are you waiting for? You have to plow the field of hatred. There, your death is sure…'"

"My soul, I am not afraid of anything. 'The land of the daffodils' is embracing us!…"

"Your words are calcined, my love, and then they turn into lava so that they can melt all the obstacles…"

"Let's go, my dear, to cool our faces down a bit in the spring. It is very hot today. Well, it is summer after all."

The big spring was close. Hand by hand, we were getting closer to it. Here there was a deeper shadow, as the old platanus with its thick branches didn't let the arrows of Apollo to go through its green belts.

"The water is ice-cold, Constantine! Let me cool you down."

"My dear, the spring is a reaction to the burning heat. Its coolness is priceless…"

"Should I bring the bag so that we can eat? I think that you should be hungry by now…"

"Here you are always hungry. The clean air, the cold water, the green grass…"

"…The calmness, the peaceful life, the tranquility arouses the hunger! Isn't this what you wanted to say," added Helen.

"Halloo Joy, Helen, so that it sets its dance in the land of rocks…"

"After eating, maybe we should sing a song, Constantine?"

"We are going to sing one of your poems. Isn't this what Palamas says: "Poem is the speech that wants to become a song"," I added.

"So let's try to turn it into a song then!" added Helen.

"… That sometimes turns into a legend or a lament!"

"What is the genuine demotic song? Have you noticed what they dance to nowadays at the festivals?"

"I have noticed. However, the demotic song has become a song, because it used to be a poem…" I noticed.

"You understand, my love, where people can take the fake poetry! There are also fake prophets. Fake prophets whose prophecies get erased with someone else's prophecies…"

"Poetry, my love is a Goddess. It never dies. They are trying to hurt it, to ridicule it, to make it disappear, but in vain. Its shapes are the same, the rest are decorations. Lamartine urges:

'Sing to the new times

the hymns of eternity!'"

"Who can listen to the eternal hymns, when around us everything is dying, everything evaporates with the strong fire and in the ashes remains their dry passion so that it can cool down with the ashes." noticed Helen with a voice that was coming out silently…

"Helen, poetry cannot be caught by anyone! We hear the poetry. It comes from a depth, it comes in the sunburnt deserts and cools us down, it quenches our thirst, gives us life, revives. You can hear its gurgle in the small pebbles of the spring, it falls down vigorously in the ravines and with its strength it drags everything useless and rotten! This is poetry. Beauty, youth, life, death, difficulties, love, passion, lust, thoughts come together and turn the thought into music, which jumps out of the nozzle of the consciousness and moves with its power and carves one road, the road of truth, of the beautiful, of the good. Poetry is redemption and the ones that are not standing reverential in front of it, turn into peels on its path. I dare to say that poetry is above that. I wouldn't hesitate to say it. I drank enough from its springs and they have made me stronger. Poetry is a rhythmic speech that makes the arrhythmias of the prose! It is a hymn of harmony and an epitaph for the people that deny it…"

"I wouldn't interrupt your 'ode' to poetry, if I didn't have something else to add," said Helen.

"Alright, love, you can say what you believe and I cannot wait to hear your definition for it."

"Dear, we can have an endless conversation about this and all definitions of poetry express a different way of being faithful to the same God. However, all of them end up there, because as you said, they all pass through the consciousness and the purpose of all of them is to find the clearness of the thoughts and the ideas as a core for the creation of the exciting poetic world. For me poetry is a melody of the chords of the soul… We will notice this in a bit, when we 'cool down' these chords and hang our guitars from the mouths of the birds…"

"Then it will stop being a lying song that wants to break the chords of poetry," I added. "We are now ready for real food," I interrupted her.

"Yes, we are."

We settled our 'table' at the cool grass, after we had put 'on lawn' all the problems that are torturing the young people and are shouting for a solution. All of a sudden we heard steps!

"Bon apetit, you enviable kids!"

"Thank you, Mr Nikos! Come near, sit down. Take a bite." with these words, Helen welcomed him.

"Thank you, children, thank you! I will just have a bit of water after the sweat dries out. My throat is all dry."

"So, Mr Nikos, what is new?" I asked.

"Nothing, Constantine. The other day we saw each other from far in the village. You are a good kid, Constantine…"

"We try to share what we have, Mr Nikos." I said.

"Exactly what you just said I learnt from my life as well. A good heart, a good person and you will never be mistaken…"

"This is an opportunity for you to tell us something." said Helen.

"You are educated kids and you would know better than I do. All I have is the weight of many more years and experience. I was even afraid to finish the two years in primary school back then. I had no inclination for learning. I regret it now. Knowledge is light. The few things I learnt though turned out to be useful."

"This is very true." said Helen.

"Yeah, well. It's all good. Life is a competition, as they say…"

"Are you coming from the village Mr Nikos?" I asked him.

"I am going to the pastures now. I am going to see my children, my sheep, my shepherds. We have the festival the day after tomorrow and I will tell them that I am going to stay with the sheep. Let them have fun as well. They are young. They may be in love. I am happy. This is it, my children, they also get tired. I share my profits with my two shepherds. Praise the Lord!"

"Praise the Lord, Mr Nikos! Because today it is the first time that we hear such good words from one good person, I jumped from happiness to greet him…"

"Don't say big words, Constantine. All of us want something good, but we get confused and make mistakes. Let me tell you my news then, as the conversation brought it and Helen is next to me. The beauty and kindness of Helen are like a copy of the ones of my late wife Maria. She never dies, my children! Everything is still alive! Do you want me to tell you the story from my youth?"

"Of course we do!" we both shouted.

"So, I was young. Ah, if youth was youth two times, as that famous demotic song says! Maria was my neighbour. I was living in my father's house. Back then Maria was going to high school, let's say, so that we don't get confused, because it was called in a different way before and in a different now. The nail pierced my heart, as you say and I was hurting, hurting a lot…"

"… Why Mr Nikos?" interrupted Helen.

"It was not her fault, the young girl! But I had the nail in my heart. I had already stopped school already and I was taking care of my property, my father's property. Maria finished high school and started preparing for exams for the University. In summer she was coming back to the village. I had abandoned all my work and I was sitting on the window that looked to her terrace. I started writing her a letter, so that I could show her how I feel about her, my love! I was so shy."

"Why, Mr Nikos?" asked Helen.

"What could I write? Many different things. I was thinking about starting from the starts, the moon, the flowers and the sweet erotic songs, but I was afraid that something will crush in my face. What had happened to me, kids!"

"And what did you do then, Mr Nikos? Did you keep sitting there just… looking at the starts?" I asked.

"You are joking, Constantine. But you are right! I was not even sure if she had understood something! I decided to go to her house one evening, because I saw her reading on her terrace. I dressed up, I combed my thick hair carefully, I looked at myself at least five or six times in the mirror until I made sure that I am worth something! And I took the road of… torture!

Maria saw me coming and she shouted: 'Nikos, come over here to keep me company!'… My beloved children, the world turned upside down… 'Come over,' she went on. We will have sone coffee as well. You have to give me poison, Maria, I whispered to myself… I went up the stairs. What a beauty. She was turning me on."

"Oh, Mr Nikos, not with these words." I noticed.

"You are right, Constantine, but I am as well. She told me to sit, I sat down. She closed her book. She was happy. The truth is that I was not sure if this was truth or a dream. We will make a coffee and drink it in peace, she said… I felt as if I got hit by thunder! I wanted to leave as soon as possible. She had figured out what was happening, I realised. I was hanging in the chair and I don't remember if my feet were touching the ground or not. I was feeling as there was no gravity. Ready to enjoy our coffee, she said. It was a torture for me. Cold sweat was running down my body and then she said: 'I am your neighbour, Nikos, and you are passing by the door and you are not talking to me. Did you forget our childhood games?' More thunder hit me! I didn't know where I took the strength from and decided to get in this 'dance' and to avoid the torture with the drop. 'We were kids back then,' I said. 'There are other thoughts that are torturing us now and unsure hopes that are tyrannising us,' I told her. 'You are right,' she said. 'You have already accepted the weight of your family and your big property. You have many worries,' she added. 'But this doesn't mean that you have to forget your friends,' she added. A third clap of thunder! The last one killed me! Was it irony or was it that her strength was growing with my weakness? To not say to much, I decided to tell her the truth straight away. It was a good opportunity anyway. I raised my eyes and the strong flames of my weakness and I said: 'Maria, I need to tell you something. I will say it so that I can get rid of the weight. You have the right to say whatever you want'… And the clap of forth thunder came! 'Thank you, Nikos,' she said. 'It is a thought that is torturing you. This is why I called you!' I had understood it. When you understand it as well one day, you will say "thank you". What you believe now may be the beginning for something better. And then you will be proud of yourself, because you came on top of the things and you caught the reality. 'That's enough, Maria,' I interrupted her. 'Thank you for your good words. It was very stupid from my side. Please forgive me! I will try to become like you. This is enough for me…' I believed her words. They were all clear and genuine like her beauty. I had to drown all these thoughts of mine. I understood that it was passion. Passion, my children, doesn't let you choose the right way. I was lost in my ways. She showed me the right, the good way. She was educated. I was just an illiterate landowner. She had dreams completely different from mine. These things though can't stop anyone loving or respecting. This is what I found in Maria. From then, Maria was my best friend and I have to tell you that I learnt a lot from her and all that I learnt was useful. And so you to have to love each other and love everyone else. I tired you a bit with the stories of my old tribulations, but what to do, we, the elder ones have an obligation to you to tell you the truth!"

"Your words are very beautiful, Mr Nikos! Words that give fruit to found souls." said Helen.

"And now excuse me for leaving you here. I need to go. However, let me tell you something about John as well. He is your friend from childhood, Constantine. However, I want to warn you that you have to be aware of what I am about to tell you now. John goes around the village drunk and keeps talking about the rocks. Mitros, next to him, but sober, is trying to calm him down. When I left, they were taking him home 'dead'!"

"What can we do, Mr Nikos?" I asked.

"Oh, my kids, 'from my pain, to the ones that are in pain' and, I am afraid… when they don't have brains!"

"Yes, but it sounds that the 'medical' advice of your late Maria has also infected you…"

"All I'm saying is this: be careful! Be careful more about Mitros! He is the devil in human body!… Ok, I am saying goodbye now."

We both remained silent for a while. After a while Maria said:

"What can we do about him, Constantine?! He is crazy!"

"The only thing that we can do is to protect ourselves from the crazy people!"

"It got a little bit windy," said Helen. "What time is it?" she asked.

"Three o'clock." I replied.

"What's happening today? A big parade here at the rocks. These rocks turned out to be very popular. One leaves, another comes," noticed Helen.

"I don't know what Hephaestus[6] is preparing in his workshop! We are only seeing the sparks now..."

"Oh God, what a world!" shouted Helen, hopelessly.

"A very beautiful world to get tortured by the devils in." I underlined.

"Leave it, leave it. We have said this many, many times. We are cleansing our own space with our own incenses." noticed Helen, melancholically.

"Whoever keeps them cleansed is a winner and doesn't need spirits and other substances so that he can find himself in an artificial paradise..."

---

1 **"Water and earth".** *With this phrase, mentioned by Herodotus, the Persians asked for the ones they were conquering to quit from all their rights on the earth and their goods. The phrase "water and earth", even in Modern Greek symbolised the subjection without limits to a conquerer.*

2 **Harpies.** *According to the Greek mythology they were female creatures with the body of a bird and a head of a woman that were the messengers of Hades. The most famous story that mentions the Harpies describes them as the punishers of the prophet Phineus (look below). Phineus was blinded by Zeus, because he was revealing his intentions to the mortals. That's why Zeus sent the Harpies to him and they were catching his food and eating it with its beaks and that's why the prophet was always hungry. The Argonauts saved him from this torture when they stopped to give him an advice when they were passing near him.*

3 **Phineus.** *Look "Harpies", "Argo", "Wandering Rocks".*

4 **Tiresias.** *In Greek mythology he was a famous all around Greece prophet from Thebes.*

In an argument between Zeus and Hera, they called Tiresias so that they can consult him, because both Gods knew that he had been both a woman and a man previously. The question they asked him was: "Who gets more pleasure in sex, the man or the woman." Tiresias answered without any hesitation: "Seven times more, the woman!' This answer angered Hera and she blinded him for punishment. Zeus then, for compensation, gave him the gift of prophecy and length of life lasting for seven generations.

5 Bulls. *This is also one of the aspects of the expedition of the Argonauts. (look also "Jason" and "Argo"). As soon as Aeetes heard that Jason was looking for the Golden Fleece, he gave him the task to yoke the bulls and plow the field with dragon teeth, so that he could give him what he wanted. The bulls that were called "the bronze bulls" had bronze hooves and fire shooting from their mouths. The bulls were a gift from the blacksmith of the God Hephaestus for king Aeetes.*

6 Hephaestus. *In Greek mythology he is the God of fire and metallurgy. He was born ugly and disabled so much, that his own mother, Hera, threw him from Olympus because she was embarrassed. The baby-God fell in the sea, where Thetis and Eurunomes picked him up and raised him for nine years.*

CHAPTER SEVEN

Memories: the last day, the last night...

It is true that the warning of Mr Nikos had worried both me and Helen a lot. All of the sudden we heard a voice from far:

"Constantine, Helen, Constantine!"

"Who is calling us, Helen?" I asked.

"It's my sister's voice. Where is she?" she asked.

I got up and I saw Alexandra looking for us down at the lakes. I ran.

"Constantine, Constantine. Where is my sister?" she asked.

"What happened, Alexandra?" I asked, worried.

"I was afraid that I am not going to find you. And the heat is filling my brain with bad thoughts. Every branch that was moving was scaring me..."

"Calm down," I told her, "Give me your hand. Let's go."

"Alexandra, my sister. What happened? What is dad doing? Is he alright?"

"Everything is alright! I just had some very bad thoughts on my mind and they wouldn't let me calm down. Nightmares, Helen, nightmares..."

"It's from the heat, Alexandra. Calm down now. Don't you start thinking that we are a part of your nightmares as well!"

"Constantine. As soon as I learnt that you came yesterday to the village I didn't want to waste any time. When I heard it, I calmed down. I am not afraid anymore."

"What happened, Alexandra?" asked Helen, worried.

"Nothing, nothing. Just let me rest for a while. Do you have a bit of water?" she asked. "I am sweating from the heat..." she added.

"Relax now and have some water…" I told her.

"How kind you are, Constantine. Why were you away for so long? Did you forget your two beloved sisters?"

"Words come out of your mouth with so much joy when you believe them!"

"Constantine, and how much joy do words have when they are accompanied by acts as their seal…"

"You proved that to me, Alexandra. I don't need anything else. How are your classes going?"

"I finished high school this year. I am studying now, preparing for the exams for University."

"Which department are you preparing for?"

"The School of Philosophy."

"Great. It is going to be our family science. Well done, Alexandra, good luck."

"When are you leaving, Constantine?"

"In three days."

"Let's leave together! It's too boring here in the land of the rocks. Only if you stay with us…" said Alexandra.

"I would love to, but I can't. The 'iron working hours' are expecting me."

"'Iron' you say?"

"Yes. It is even the softer way to say it." I said.

"Why?" asked Alexandra.

"Because, as a worker. you are forced to stay for the arranged working hours even if you don't have anything to do."

"So what do you want to do?" she asked.

"My own scientific work! I want to be free. I want to read, research, write, comment, discover…" I said.

"So, if I got this right, your wish is to have an academic career?" asked Alexandra.

"Wishing is not enough. You also need to try hard." I noted.

"You are scaring us, Constantine. Now when we have started to get used to your presence, we will miss you even more when you leave again." she added.

"But it will be continued in Athens, Helen."

"Athens looks like a dream to me," said Helen."I don't know what has gotten over me, but I miss it so much. When are we going to leave, Constantine?"

"We will arrange to leave on August the 16th…"

"Tell us, Alexandra, why did you come to the rocks?" asked Helen.

"I couldn't wait for you. I just went home, sat for a while and got ready, even though father told me not to come, because I was tired. I wanted to see Constantine, the good boy! My brother, Constantine. And also, the son of Costoulas pissed me off."

"John?" asked Helen.

"Yes, John. He sent Mitros yesterday - why are you shaking your head - with one letter, one note with which he was asking me to have a 'relationship' with him and which I ripped up straight away. 'I am rich,' he was saying, 'and you are the woman of my dreams! You have to give me an answer, because I am melting,' he was saying. These are the things I remember the most, because they made me laugh the most. I am afraid of him though, my siblings, I am really afraid of him. This is why I came so quickly to the rocks…"

"Constantine! What are you going to say about this?" asked Helen, worried.

"Nothing more than what Alexandra said. Father of daemons, until when are you going to torture the human souls?"

"I bet that he has gone mad. He will do something really bad." predicted Helen. "Because after he was harassing me for so long with his talks about love and relationships, now he started doing the same to you. And what did you reply to him, sis?"

"What do you want me to say? Straight forward - to leave me alone and spend more time with his sheep!"

"A very good answer." I replied.

"Don't be scared, Alexandra. It is the drunkness, it will go away…"

"He is an idiot and he will remain an idiot!"

"It is not good, Alexandra, to talk like this. Is he responsible for his stupidity? He is just a child of bad parents."

"Have you eaten?" asked Alexandra.

"Just now. We just finished eating and were about to start singing." answered Helen. "The chorus is even bigger now."

"What are we going to sing?" asked Alexandra.

"It's my poem." said Helen.

"Which one?"

"The song of love!"

"Good! Let's go:

Now when the clouds

chose the oblivion

and the birds of memory flew over,

I will sit with them for a while

in the blossoms of your soul,

I will sing for us.

You showed up in the garden

as if the biggest of the lilies

and the knock of love

you gave to them."

"An angelic song, incense in the skies and an 'eternal hymn', when am I going to hear you again?" I enquired, commenting on the 'song of love'.

"Did you start your comment, Constantine?" interrupted Helen.

"Yes, and I will continue now, Helen! And if the branches of hatred have sealed its heart, and they opened to the eternal and infinite skies of love. You got bored of the land of the rocks, but for them you sacrificed your youth, so that the hymn could come out and rip the curtains off!... The rocks, I was careful of the rocks. After a hand decorated with lilies was pushing me to their base, I raised my eyes to see that the big rocks are pushing down and your song is hypnotising me, when my being is all shaken by the fall of the rocks. And I can always hear your voice: 'Constantine, Constantine!' It brings me near you, like we were back then that afternoon, the three of us."

"Constantine, your 'prophecies' are scaring me!...When are we going to leave?" asked Helen, thoughtfully.

"Why, dear, are you rushing the chariot of time? He is throwing molecules and we are collecting sparkles in our palms. We will leave. We have prepared already. Let's go."

We took the flat road, so that we could go home more quickly. We were tired walking on the mud paths.

"How sweet is the moment of return? Even though the tiredness and nostalgia make the body feel heavier…"

"The Homeric 'sweet return'[1]? The sweet day of return?" asked Helen.

"Yes, but in a shorter version!"

"Same as the 'ascending smoke'[2], the smoke that ascends from the chimney of home, is the end of the nostalgic return!"

"It is, Constantine, a sign that something is alive." added Helen.

"For me, dear, it is a sign that something dark is happening!… We left behind the 'ascending smoke' while Odysseus was looking for a chimney. That was the good thing about his home."

"Is this the interpretation you are giving, Constantine?" asked Helen, puzzled.

"I bet you that there is no other. The smoke is the martyr of the fire."

"I understood your cycle! Now you have imprisoned me forever." noticed Helen.

"No! We wished to come in because we found it right! The bigger the sum of circles, the better, more real and stronger is the 'so that'." I said.

The walk brought us to the yard. We got there before even realising. We came into the house. Mr Vassilis was waiting for us with impatience and joy.

"Welcome, welcome, kids from the garden of your youth," he said with relief. "Did you have fun, Constantine?" he asked me.

"Yes, we did, daddy," Helen rushed to say. "Great. You stayed alone for a while. And now the house is full again." she said and jumped towards her father so that she could kiss him.

"All the best, kids, all the best," he said with joy. "I want to sit in the garden. The sun is setting slowly. Let's go outside."

We freshened up and we sat on the chairs outside.

"Did you find the old Mitros, Constantine?" asked Mr Vassilis. "You know that he is a skunk and a liar?"

"Yes, we found him." I said.

"We found him, dad," added Helen, "We found him and I told him about the lamb. He is going to bring it to us tomorrow. We will meet him at the rocks tomorrow morning and we will come back."

"So you will go again tomorrow morning?" asked Mr Vassilis.

"We will go for a walk again tomorrow morning, the three of us, and we will come back quickly." said Helen.

"Alright, Helen, alright. You should go together, thankfully Constantine is here as well because I am afraid of Mitros."

A soft breeze was coming from the gulf and was becoming stronger when the fire sphere was reaching the cushions of the mountains. It was going through the branches of the trees that started wavering, it was caressing the overheated leaves and was resting in the gold hairs of the girls as if it wanted to settle its throne forever in their curls. Everything was breathing deeply so that it could accept the arrival of a new colour. In the twilight you could see the complaint that lasts as long as you need so that you can get used to a new one. It is the forecourt of a sacramental space. Going inside you could see all the serpents that woke up from darkness, carve in the soft soil their passage with their dragging, as if they are drawing the knit of the burning rivers of hell. Their eyes are phosphorescing in the moulded corners, trying to give life to the land of the werewolves. They start showing up first hesitantly, later on bravely and dig messages, knock down ivies, surround rocks and stand on the rocks like barkers of a dae-monic smell. The moon could carve their route with a hedge with its blurry rays or to make the moonlight to bubble even more from its passion.

"Are you not sleeping, Constantine?" asked Helen with concern because she could see that I was thoughtful and worried. The night is a willing slave of the blurred thought. It gives it its black apron, it gives it the knot and offers it as a gift to the soul. When it unties, it gets all excited from the grubby parts of its flesh and gets poisoned. The chirping of the birds unbury its body that in the morning light imagines the worms of the dungs.

"Darling, the night could not take you away from my eyes, because you are not made of pieces of a slave's apron. Neither the rest of the nights succeeded to take you away. The dawn in spite of the night, from the pruning hook of time, cuts the succulents sprouts and makes with them its vast bed."

"Constantine, your 'prophecies' are scaring me," interrupted Helen upset. "They have always scared me because they were always true."

"We need many tombs so that we can see how far human tastes go. We are putting it in front of our noses and we step on it with our feet. Does one need to break the tombstones so that he can take Arete[3] from afar? Then the birds of consciousness remain to uncover with their voices the steps of death."

"Constantine, I repeat, you are scaring me! Go to bed now. Get rid of the bad thoughts. Imagine that this is… the previous night!"

She came close to me. She hugged me, she kissed me. I hugged her, I kissed her. We were in the skies!… And then… she disappeared behind the walls of the house with her flimsy spider web night dress that made her look like an angel.

I couldn't sleep. Like the previous night, she said. But how many nights run after the dawns with their hair down so that they can jump with rage in the sea of eternity? I dare to say that I have counted them. I found them, I found them in the garden of Gethsemane, in every Gethsemane, in every rocky land. And later on the Resurrection. Ah, if only I could, black night, turn your apron into a shroud in the empty grave! But what am I saying! I hear a voice saying "Hello". And I fall at your sweet feet, calm idol: Love!

My eyes are blurring. At the place I am, a piece of earth immovable by its turns, the night covered you and the eyes of my soul accompany you in your sleep. You gave me your dream and I presented you my eternal dawn. The hands have been made to hold the rivers of pain, the eyes to look at the fire of hell, the lips to mourn the human ruins and the ears to hear the cut breaths at lives cut at their own feet. And above all these remains one voice of hope:

Suck the nights

the dawns to strengthen!

I sucked the night, the first nightingale and in its juices I found the enemy of the blossom that was fooling it with its poisonous tongue. Now the fatigue seals its eyes so that a world remains, a world that is not closing in the close of the eye, but a world that opens its gates to the Zephyr[4] of the real life. The beautiful, the nice, the light, the clear. The earth is not being held by the rocks and the watts. It's been held by the blue sky. The earth is holding graves, Centaurs[5], Harpies, Ephialtes... And when it is filled with them, one Hieron[6] reaches to bring them up to date! The human is the biggest weakness of the human, like the sleep for the dream!...

Dear, I left you in the garden bathed by the moon, so that the dream can wash you...

---

1 "The sweet return". *A phrase in the Odysseus of Homer, meaning the sweet day of the return home, in the homeland...*

2 "The ascending smoke". *A Homeric phrase for the desire of the person left outside at night to see even from afar the ascenting smoke from his house's chimney...*

3 Arete. *A tragic heroine in the "Song of the dead brother", which belongs to common traditions that are connected to the ethnic beliefs. This song is one of the most important ones for the creations of the greek demotikh.*

4 Zephyr. *In Greek mythology he is the personification of the west wind, that continues to be called with the same name even today. It is a soft wind that cools down the Elysian Fields and helps in vegetation.*

5 Centaurs. *Creatures from Greek mythology. In history and art they are shown as anthropomorphous, with half a human body on the top, and half a horse body.*

6 Hieron. *He is an important part of the Greek mythology, as much as for his connection with therapy and other physical sciences in the Ancient world, as with his connection with the education of the heroes. He is presented in many myths with most important the one in which he is mentioned to be Achilles' teacher.*

CHAPTER EIGHT

Memories: The last nightmare of Helen

But so, I didn't have time to close my eyes:

"Be careful; be careful of the rocks, Constantine! Constantine, where are you?"

"What happened, dear, so that you are ripping off the bowels and the black veil of the night with your voice? Which dream sucked your sweet sleep and left you without a drop of peace?"

I jumped up and I said all these trembling. Alexandra, who was sleeping next to Helen, woke up as well. Shaken from the depths of her sleep, she couldn't believe that she was awake…

"What happened, sister?" asked Alexandra in the night.

"A bad dream was pressing my soul and I can't breath…"

I sat next to her. Her heart was beating loudly, cold sweat was running down her face and her eyes started to come out of the land of the unreal. I covered her, because the night wind was blowing as if it was jealous of her angelic face. Her rich hair was damp from the night battle…

"I woke you up! But it is not my fault. Bad omens in the black sheet of the night, decorated by the dreams. My feet feel weak. I can't believe that it was all a dream!"

"Calm down, darling. The morning wind is going to clear the footprints of the night and the serpents will go back to their dark corners." I said, trying to calm her down.

"Don't come with us to the rocks, Constantine! I am afraid."

"How can I take your soul from the Zephyrs and leave it to the daemons, dear?"

"No, no! I can not let Zephyr go away from my sight. The eyes of the night have a catastrophic strength," said Helen, somehow calmer.

"Why, Helen, are you looking at this force? Your strength is bigger than the one that rocks have. They are trembling. That's why their base is squeaking. Is this strength?"

"Darling, leave my thoughts, as they are a continuation of others that the shadow of the rocks has planted. I don't want to heal my thoughts with sleep. Yours, as they are a shelter, are enough. How much of the night has passed and how much is left?" she asked with questioning eyes.

"What has passed is left. But why are you asking? I will hallo the Lucifers and will bring the stars down to your mattress so that they can shine next to you."

"Are you going to tell us what your dream was, sis?" asked Alexandra.

"I will tell you. What can I be afraid of anyway when I have Constantine in my arms and my sister near me. Am I right?"

"And so you are going to take him with you to the rocks, to the top of the nightmare cave?" I asked.

Alexandra laughed. She wanted to say something. At first she swallowed it, but at the end she couldn't hold herself and she said:

"How can you be joking in this moment, Constantine?"

"It is just a dream, Alexandra, just a dream! It takes you wherever it wants. With invisible bridles made in Hephaestus' workshop…"

"… To whom we give iron so that he can put it on our necks and leashes taken from the old basement of our subconscious." added Helen.

"… That reptilians bring from its windows!"

"Oh, we started to rub the deep night dreams with the millstones of the thoughts," said Alexandra, who didn't want to get involved in the topic of the 'prophetic' discussions.

"Alright!" said Helen. "We are stopping our 'rubbing'. I will tell you about the night visit I had. Oh God, all these visions are becoming alive in front of my eyes! So, we were sitting at the big spring, exactly where Alexandra found us. We were singing my 'love song' and then all of the sudden the sides of the rocks started to stretch even higher, their top started reaching further and then their foundation just broke into two. A massive giant was covering the whole of the valleys with his shadow and at the top the last sun ray was shutting down. We looked like ants next to him. Our lips were sealed, the stones were melting under his steps and his laughter - this horrible, miserable laugh! It made the bodies of the trees bend. Stone hands were going up and down and the eyes were throwing burning lava coming from his guts. And he was shouting: "Son of my enemy, how dare you touch my bleeding feet? How dare you lay in my murdering arms? Son of my enemy, love!" The valley was screaming and the bay dried out from fear. We remained as stones and you, Constantine, shouted: "My enemy, in your stone chest I have scattered soil from my soul, so that I can turn you into a garden! Ha ha ha! You son of the evil down, I will turn you into a small stone part in my soul." And straight away he reached out with his arm! And then I couldn't hold myself anymore and I screamed! I screamed so that the night could hear me. Ah, I can't, I can't..."

"Son of the illusion, dream that gets Morpheus[1] drunk, what other lie, bigger than this could you give birth to?" I said.

Alexandra was shaking from fear and with a voice that was trembling, she said:

"If I knew that it was that scary, I wouldn't ask you to tell us your dream, sis! Constantine, I am afraid! My feet are trembling, my hands as well, my whole body is trembling!"

"It is trembling from the strength of the... giant!" I tried to calm her down.

"Ah, endless night, that you feed of insomnia and rotten dreams, when do you end?" said Helen.

"Calm down, dear! The treadles stopped at the margins of your soul."

"And I can hear your voice that sounds like the voice of a nightingale!"

We were pushing the hours away with our words and they were pulling us into our dens so that they can show us to their diabolic allies. The rocks were standing silently. They were changing shapes in front of my eyes so that they could hide the rats within their curves. In the stove of the night they were making their tools and they were holding the spring in their hands, so that they could hurt it. My imagination was galloping towards dark places where I could hear only gasps and see only full graves. But she was inviting me next to her, so that I could hold her hands, to turn off the fire that was burning from her dream and to hold her in my strong hands.

"Let's go, my dear, let's go far from the masses of rocks," Helen was saying, "Let's go far away to where life is growing, our new life. It is all death here!"

"Why are you afraid of the rocky hills, dear, now when they are so ugly?" I asked.

"How many crosses buried in its body does Golgotha want until its tombs all open?" shouted Helen upset and with a mind heavy from bad thoughts.

"Take away your nets, daughter of hell, and stop hiding the light." I shouted. "My feet are fast, I will force the hours to jump in the chasm!"

"What happened to you, Constantine?" asked Helen. "The sun is killing the night made from mould."

"Crystal voice, you are calling me into the eternal river of life. I am driving away the nights from the rocks with your torch in hand. Their last black flakes writhe in the light and their feet tremble. It is leaving, it is leaving together with its slaves. Here we go; they are wearing their day clothes!"

"Daughter with rose lips, why are you giving your hands so hesitantly? Is it because you dislike how we got scared by the ugly teeth of the night for a while?" asked Helen angrily.

"My dawn, it probably got jealous of you because you survived the pressure of the night. One beauty always throws its jealousy at another beauty."

"Lets leave it like that then, support of my youth, immortal ivy." said Helen, looking at the rose-fingered aurora. "Kids, it's time to get ready."she said. "The giant took our sleep anyway."

I was getting ready as my angel said this. The sun stood still at the cheeks of the horizon and then started moving higher in the sky. Life hugs one more time the dew drops and looks at its reflection in the drizzled vines. The fruit becomes sweeter and sweeter as it sucks the sun rays, the rays of matureness, its unripe taste. Nature opens its colourful wings and greets the new light. Only the rocks remain all naked with their fake indifference. It's time to roost. The night is for them what day is for the rest that dare to look at its light. There is only one hope left. And then I heard the same voice:

Suck the nights

the dawns to strengthen!

How many times are we going to hear it, so that it will stop us from falling where the stones are rolling down? In their fall they open one pit first for them and then for the rest that will sit in their ridge like eternal barkers of distraction and hatred.

The giants are wounded, their cruel laughters are sealed with earth from their own soil, their bloody hands are cut off and are jammed in their body and the huge, flesh-filled teeth are falling in their stone field, so that they never spring up or to spring up the fire breathing dragons of Jason. This is the night with its werewolves. The imaginary fig tree becomes dry and its branches turn into bows for their enemies. A fire face that melts the irons of Hephaestus and with it Olympus fears the hatred.

Today again we will climb the rocks, we will look down from up there. A walk in the land of the daffodils. There, where the snoring of the springs never stops, as if it is telling us that life gets cleaned by the soil that brings it back more cool, more clean than its insides.

The morning coffee under the vines uncovered how we sucked the black night without taking a breath and on top of its sizzle we saw its bad moods…

"What happened last night? You turned the night into day? As if we are not going to see each other again!" said Mr Vassilis when he came out in the garden.

"Do you want me to make you a coffee, daddy?" asked Helen.

"Ok, let me have a coffee with you for a company. But only if it is not bitter! What is happening, Constantine?" he said to me, patting me on the shoulder.

"Good morning, Mr Vassilis." I said to distract him. "How are you today?"

"I was keeping my 'Good morning' to say when my coffee arrives. But you were faster..."

"We have to say 'Good morning', because we are tired of having the night." I said

"Leave this, Constantine. I can't stand the game of words. The other day you gave me a headache or, even more, a migraine with your words. Tell me what you want to tell me clear and white. I am not from the... School of Philosophy!"

"What will someone get if he goes to the rocks running? He will get tired and he won't see anything." I said, because I wanted to end the conversation.

"You started the same again! I told you, your words and arguments are nice, but I don't want this... dizziness !"

"Then can I offer you a hot... coffee?" I asked.

"I will accept that." said Mr Vassilis.

"Daddy, should I go with them to the rocks to get the lamb?"

"You are all acting as if you are going to get the Erymanthian Boar. It is just an innocent lamb ready for slaughter. However, I suggest that one of you stays here. It is a bad hour, you see. You should not go somewhere all together. You never know what might happen. I didn't want to say it, but I am afraid for you."

"It sounds like I finished, so that you can start." I noticed. "However, your fears are a characteristic thing for all parents that love their children too much."

"Anyway. When are you going?"

"We are climbing… Golgotha in a bit." I said.

"Ah, shut up, Constantine! What is all this? Soon you will tell me that you will climb Caucasus[2] as well."

We closed the gate to the yard after Mr Vassilis wished us good luck and we took the path that was taking us to the place, 'The sheep Manina' as the locals call it. From there we would cut a bit sideways and we would climb the rocks. They are a bit far, but, as we were the three of us, the road didn't look long for us. We could find there Mitros or John.

The three of us continued slowly down the path. It was the last time that I would climb the rocks with Helen!…

---

1 Morpheus. *In Greek mythology he was considered the God of sleeping and dreams. He was presented with winds that were so strong and flexible, that they could take him to the end of the world. It is worth mentioning that the drug morphine took its name from Morpheus.*

2 Caucasus. *Look at "Prometheus".*

CHAPTER NINE

A sudden interruption of memories:
The tragedy at the rocks

We arrived. We sat at some stones to rest and all of the sudden we saw John Costoulas to sit on a rock a bit further than us. He was waiting for us!

"Why didn't you tell me that Costoulas was coming as well? Now I feel like I want to run, to go back… Don't you see how he is sitting on the rock as a crow? Don't you see how his eyes throw burning lava? Did you do it on purpose?" demanded Alexandra, angrily.

"We didn't think about it, Alexandra. But anyway, why do you care? Why are you afraid of the crow, when you know where he is?" I asked.

"I can't, I can't look at him, Constantine."

"You are right, Alexandra." I said. "You should make him suffer even more with your light, to tremble under your eyes, to choke from your acts and burn from your words! As if nothing happened. Ok?"

"I was not expecting instead of a lamb, to find a… crow!" said Helen.

"The lamb will come as well to the wolf's shoulders." I answered.

"Constantine, the crows wait for food from the wolves. The wolf is sucking the blood and the crow is tearing the leftovers."

"He is looking at us from up there," I said to the girls. "Don't look at him. Let's sit here and discuss this."

"Yes, Constantine, let's sit down. Up there it smells like carrion." said Alexandra, who didn't want to stop.

"You, Alexandra, should look happy all the time when we are up there. Don't frown, but destroy his cloudiness with your light. He might feel sorry for all this! He didn't even do any crime. He just wrote a very bad love letter. Anyway, he received one good and correct answer. And what does his passion for Helen mean? We should always think about the consequences of an act. All the rest we put it into the 'archive'. Do you hear me, Alexandra?" I shouted.

"Thank you, Constantine, for your good and wise words. This is the best that I could do. Anything else would have the opposite effect..."

"Exactly! Everyone loves himself because of their acts and reacts to the same rays that hit the mirror and come back..."

"What you just said, I have noticed in Helen as well. She faces things in the same way. Always calm and welcoming, always a clear sky that doesn't fear lightnings."

"She is my soul mate!"

"John looks very thoughtful. Do you see it?" said Helen.

"Maybe he is preparing something, Helen." I said. "Maybe some excuse for the surprise he got. Be careful though, we don't know anything..."

"Can he believe something like that?" asked Alexandra.

"We will make him believe, Alexandra." I said. "Only like this we could put it in the vortex of his rotten thoughts..."

"Let's go up a bit and say hi." said Helen.

We climbed the ascent and came near to him.

"Hello and all the best, John!"

As if he was surprised or he acted as he was surprised. He raised his head high and he didn't say a word. Later on he put his head down and he dived in his thoughts. Love or madness?

"Good morning, John." we greeted again.

Helen ran towards him, so did Alexandra.

"But what's wrong with you today, you are being so silent? As if your eyes have been drowned in a misty sea so that they can not see foamy waves." I said.

"…Insomnia, my friends! I couldn't close my eyes last night."

"Then you can appreciate more the price and the importance of sleep." I noticed.

"Not when you are offering it, my friend."

"I, however, don't get tired of finding the importance in your thoughts! You are offering it to me without even understanding. This is the difference…"

"We have a lot of differences, we two."

"Differences deep and high."

"Let me make it easier for you: differences in depth and height"

"Stop this, kids!" intervened Helen. "These things can have only one conclusion: hatred."

"No. We haven't reached there yet, Helen. At least I don't want to go there. John and I were just talking to pass the time."

"I don't know, I don't know what thread is pulling me and taking me where it wants to." said bitterly John.

"I think that you are pulling a thread and it just wouldn't stretch more." I replied. "If you keep pulling it you will rip it off and it will leave you rolling down the stones!"

"Shut up, Constantine," he said with a strong reaction. "Don't bury my brain even more. What are these knives that you are throwing at me?"

He jumped up, tightened his hands, clenched his teeth. How could he find the truth that was constantly uncovering him? Which force would stand by him, to take off the giant parts of his soul? The Wandering Rocks spread death amongst the weak ones. Without the white dove, where do you go you root of nettle? Find the magic wand to become a pig in Circe's garden![1] You can't do even that? Then why are you shouting and looking for the palace?

There is an image of a Centaur in the wild rocks. But does Heracles need to kill the Nessus?[2] May be they as well don't let their blood black from the hits to shed death with their vapours? Yes, but there are Nessus in the land of Phidares[3]! Others will descent in the land with deep shadows. Can you hear their clatters?

"Why are you so silent, my friends?" said Helen.

"I can hear kits, sledgehammers, spades, hoes, suffocated voices, spears, bows, falling at the hills of the mountains." I said allegorically.

"What poisonous arrows are you throwing at me today so that I wish this day didn't come?" asked John nervously.

"… The works of night, the day can see and laughs at them." I replied.

"Shut up at last, you devil! Stop hurting my soul." he said.

"I don't understand you, my friend." I said. "Your anger is hiding something bad. What is happening that is making you angry?"

"Ah, I cannot stand your words anymore! Leave me alone to do some thinking."

"But what is happening here?" said Helen. "Are you feeling alright, John? Tell us, John, tell us even if it is something very bad." she said and caressed his hair.

"Wind, blow so that you can cool down my soul. Why are you siting, my enemies, and you are making fun of me?" he shouted.

"Shut up, John, stop it! You need to calm down. We have to go to the village. The heat is bothering him." said Helen.

Helen was holding his hand. He was standing at the same rock where we found him as a drunk person. Deep darkness, how you spread to cover the light! But somewhere, somewhere exists a flame that lightens the darkest corners. But you pall your smoke! You give strength, you take weakness. You give courage, they make you kneel. What remains standing? You dry the spring of your soul and throw its water to the unquenchable holes. Where is the drop? Thirsty wasps are searching in the dry mouth by habit and they are even more thirsty. Look at their flight! Shake the empty branches so that their fruits that were ironising from afar will fall on the earth. And their hands are dragging on the sharp rocks to find a stall. It is enough for them to hold for a while their weight and then they fall. They are coming, the workers of the night, with a lamb on their shoulder!

I don't know why everyone remained with their own trail of thoughts. We were sitting silently on the rocks. It was like the calm before the storm. Helen next to Alexandra was sitting with a distant face in a never-ending thought. In the end there is no solution. The end is an illusion that is pulling you towards it. And when you get there, what is eating for you? One other thread for someone else…

Mitros was one… end of my thoughts. Some thread was pulling him and pulling him. The rocks were the end! I was flooded with thoughts and I shouted, breaking the weird silence:

"Mitros is coming as well. He is bringing the lamb for slaughter."

"It was time to break a bit the silence. Mitros is coming, the bearer of evil." said Helen.

"… and of many sufferings." added Alexandra to what Helen had just said.

"But, Ostas, there are many more sufferings that come from your words." said John.

"What value do words have compared to deeds, Costoulas?" I said.

In the meantime Mitros had come near.

"Hello, Mitros." I said.

"Hello, boys and girls. I am a bit late, so please forgive me. However, I brought you the lamb. You see, I haven't forgotten about you…"

"Sit down, Mitros, have a rest," I told him. "In a bit we are leaving for the village…"

"So quickly?" he said deviously and looked at John. "Don't go yet, I want to enjoy your company for a while. Let's climb the rocks. We will have a look from the top, smoke a cigarette and then…"

"There is a then?" I asked.

"Yes, we can throw pebbles down." he said quickly. "When I was young I was throwing big stones from the top and it made me really happy to watch them roll down! Then we can leave. Don't be afraid of the heat. I will bring the lamb for Mr Vassilis right to your door. What else do you want?! Get up, John!"

"But what happened to you today and you are acting like this?" I asked John.

"Not only today! Yesterday was the same." said Alexandra.

"I don't know about yesterday. I see him today being all cloudy. Come on, John, get up, son of the master Costoulas." I told him.

"I feel that my feet are heavy like a plumb and my brain is all blurry. I can't get up, I feel dizzy." said John.

"Ok then, leave it." I told him quickly. "Even the ladies are watching you…"

"Alright then, as you wish." he said.

"Of course they want to. What's wrong with you? You are young kids." said Mitros.

"Let us all climb and Constantine can go for water." suggested Helen.

"No, we are not going to climb on the rocks. Yesterday we climbed." I said.

"Ah, don't louse our hearts, Ostas," Mitros jumped in. "We will all go together. Do me the favour." Mitros insisted.

"Dust in the eyes maybe?" I asked.

"I said something and you took it for granted, Constantine! Come on, let's go."

"Be careful though! We don't want anything bad to happen to us. These are stones and they can start rolling down. Be careful, it's slippery." I said

"Ah, for Christ's sake! We are not children." said Mitros with joy and with a smile that showed both of his hollow teeth…

"Go forward, John. Take Alexandra by the hand and I am going to take Helen and then we can go!"

"So I am going to be by myself." said Mitros with laughter.

"The rocks are used to you…"

"I just said it for a joke. It sounds as if we are climbing Zaloggos[4]! Only that we are not singing 'be healthy, springs'." I added.

"Stop it, Constantine, please!… Your words are scaring me. I fear… I fear the giant." said Helen.

"These words I say without thinking. An invisible force is pulling them out of my mouth so that the wind can hear them." I replied.

We were walking. John was in the front with Alexandra. Mitros in the middle and me and Helen behind. John had found himself all of the sudden. Is it possible that the white hand of a girl can cool down a burning soul? Maybe the satisfaction of one such temporary 'triumph' puts the foundations for other hopes with no enemies? But then, what kind of a 'triumph' that is? You thirsty man, how do you mix up hopes with evil and dirty thought!

"Be careful, Constantine, be careful!" whispered Helen to me.

"We are almost there. The descent is more dangerous." I added.

Tired and sweaty, we reached the top. Mitros was breathing quickly.

"Ah, kids, I am very tired! The ascent is a heavy thing…"

"This is where the brave man is showing, Mitros, not down there with the canes."

"You are right, Constantine!" he said. "This is why I am going to throw a lot of pebbles down there! I am going to throw them from the place I used to when I was a child!… Come, let me show you!"

"Why are you rushing, Mitros? There are pebbles here as well! They will not run away." said John.

"Where are they going to go? The biggest pebble I will throw right now! Come and see!"

We followed Mitros. He stopped. He took us to a further place, where sharp rocks were ending in the soil. On top of it there was a huge rock that, if you were not careful, was shaking when you touch it!

"Don't be afraid," Mitros tried to calm us down. "Since I was a child, this rock was shaking, but it never ever falls down! From here I was throwing the stones. I want you to see how they fall!…"

One was not able to look down. I didn't understand what strange force had brought us there! I was getting dizzy from the big height. Mitros was shaking the big sharp rock…

"So, kids, I will show you where to sit, so that you feel safe." he said. "Constantine should go in the front because he is shorter than John and he can see how the stones are rolling down. Then John and after - Helen and Alexandra. As soon as I put the pebble at the edge of the rock, Constantine will step further to see how nicely it falls! Did we understand? I am ready!"

And so Mitros rolled the rock. I was in the front to see the nice… fall! And then! Ah, memories, don't wake up, such moments… Even I don't know how the eyes have forgotten about their light!… Don't wake up, memories, don't…

---

1 Circe. *A famous witch in Greek mythology. She lived on a faraway island Aeaea, in a marvellous palace built in a beautiful forest. With a lot of amenity she charmed Odysseus' friends and after she offered them food and magic herbs so that they forget about their homeland, she turned them into pigs with her magic wand.*

2 Nessus. *In Greek mythology Nessus was a Centaur, who established himself at the river Evinos (also called Phidares) where he was working as a ferryman, carrying travellers to the other side of the river on his back. There, many years later, Nessus met Heracles for a second time, when he was there with Deianeira. Heracles passed the river swimming, but trusted Nessus to carry her over. Nessus though attempted to kidnap Deianeira (or according to another version to rape her) and this is why Heracles killed him, killed him with his poisonous arrows (according to another version, hitting him with his bat). However, while he was dying, Nessus gave to Deianeira one magic potion that was mixed with his blood/ or his sperm, saying that if Heracles ever stopped loving her, she had to give him to wear a dress soaked in this liquid. After some time, this is what happened, when Deianeira wanted to make the hero to forget Iole: she sent to Heracles a chiton soaked with the potion. The "chiton of Nessus" was the murder weapon that killed the greatest hero in Greek mythology, who died in terrible pains.*

3 Phidares. *Look above "Nessus".*

4 Zaloggos. *One of the historical sited of Greece. It is located north of Preveza and belongs to the mountain range of the Cassiopeia of Epeiros. It's name is connected to the pre-revolutionary period of 1821 and more specifically with the famous Dance of Zaloggos. After the conquest of the area from Ali Pasha on December 18th, 1921, the Greek women that had escaped to the rocks chose instead of the dishonour and captivity to throw their children from the rocks and after that, dancing, to jump one after another from the cliff.*

CHAPTER TEN

Erinyes are persecuting the responsible for the tragedy

"Helen, Heeelen!" I was shouting. I woke up! My heart was beating as loud as drums. My eyes were blurry. I woke up. I understood. The memories brought me back twelve years ago with the barks of a strange dream. They brought me back to the rocks where I lost my Helen. Ah, my angel! The memories were fluttering and left me where I was two hours ago, in the garden of my house today with the walls covered by honeysuckle and shady vines. With grey hair and with my wife Alexandra and my ten year old daughter Helen, my Helen!

"Here I am, daddy! Did you call me?" she ran to me to answer, my little Helen, my daughter…

"Yes, baby! I just wanted a glass of water."

"Why, daddy, are you looking at me so sadly and with pain in your heart?" asked little Helen.

"Nothing, Helen. You help me relax from a very long reading of a new book…"

"Constantine, should I make you a coffee?" asked my wife Alexandra.

"Yes, darling. Thank you very much."

"Here you go, daddy, your water."

"Thank you, thank you, my heart."

"Daddy, when are we going to go to the… rocks?" asked little Helen.

"We will go, one day will go. We will go, go play now."

"Are we going to the village? It is the festival tomorrow." added little Helen.

"Ok, ok. Go play now…"

"Constantine, when did the mayor tell you that he is coming?" asked Alexandra.

"At seven, Alexandra, at seven in the afternoon. What time is it now?" I asked.

"It is five now." said Alexandra. "Did he tell you why he wants to talk to you?"

"I have no idea. However, from his half-words I understood that he wants to tell me something about Costoulas' property."

"Did I interrupt your reading?" she asked.

"No, not at all." I said to Alexandra, who looked somehow upset. "Come, sit next to me."

"Where did you find this notebook these papers?" she asked. "You, dear Constantine are going to suffocate in this paper."

"I am suffocating in my thoughts, Alexandra. These papers have a voice, have a soul…"

"But these are our Helen's, my sister's. I just remembered." said Alexandra excitedly. "These are her poems! And I left you by yourself for such a long time."

"No, not by myself! Her presence always accompanies me, her voice, her smile, her angelic face, her…"

"…Stop it, Constantine! Stop it…" said Alexandra with a tear as a hot drop coming out of her eye. "Stop it, don't make my thought so painful…"

"I always hear her voice, Alexandra: the rocks, the rocks…"

"Please, calm down! Your face is pale and your eyes are throwing sparkles…"

"…Who is coming?" I asked.

"Let me check." said Alexandra.

"Is it the mayor?" I asked.

"No, no, it is Mitros!"

"Mitros? He is coming again to the… rocks?" I asked. "What would the scorpion want?" I asked myself.

"Good evening, bosses." said Mitros. "Forgive me, Mr Ostas, for coming without warning."

"Come in, Mitros. What happened?"

"I was with my sheep nearby and I decided to come by to see you as soon as I learnt that you were here." he said.

"You did well." I said. "Would you like to have a coffee? A drink, a lemonade, what would you like?"

"One… poison if you could give me…"

"…Something is wrong and is torturing you, Mitros." I noticed.

"One coffee, Mrs Alexandra, one bitter coffee I would like." he said.

"Whatever you want, our old friend." said Alexandra.

"Sit down so that we can catch up. We have years and years to talk. How is your work going, the sheep? I heard that now you have sheep of your own."

"Yes, Professor. I have a few, around forty. What am I compared to you?! Rubbish. But you became important, I hear, you became a professor in the University! You are worthy, Mr Ostas. Not rich, but honest and hard-working and a good person! A professor in the University. You read a lot. This is why you flourished… I am just one… shepherd."

"Everyone is useful in their own job, Mitros." I replied. "Some less, some more. Some like this, some like that…"

"I will tell you something, Constantine," he said. "I cannot hide the torture in my soul anymore. This ravine is my witness and the rocks are always 'digging' into my brain…"

"…But what is happening to you, my good friend?" I said.

"Many, nightmares, wild thoughts! I don't know where to start and where to end. I will say it silently, so that your wife Alexandra doesn't hear." he added.

"Whatever you want. I am listening to you." I said.

"Put your palms on your eyes so that you cannot see me." he said with a trembling voice. "I cannot face you otherwise."

"Alexandra, leave the coffee here." I said to my wife, who was bringing the coffee to Mitros. "Please leave us alone for a while." I asked.

"Ok, Constantine. I will go with my daughter Helen for a walk."

"Very good, dear, a very good idea!"

"I just heard now the name 'Helen', your daughter's name and as if thunder fell in my soul." said Mitros. "How much does she look like the late Helen!" he went on. "When I look at Alexandra it is breaking my heart."

"What can we do, Mitros. Everything happens… by chance."

"What 'chance', Mr Constantine! Everything happens because the devil decides. It is all our fault and we throw it at fate! I… I… I…"

"…So?…"

"If the earth could only open and swallow me. This is where I belong. In the earth, in the earth, Mr Ostas!"

"I don't understand you, Mitros! Have you been drinking?" I asked.

"No, I'm telling the truth, even though it comes from my broken heart." he said. "I will say it though, I will say it, so that I can get rid of it!"

"Say it, Mitros, say it, if it is true as you say."

"Where we are now, here, twelve years ago, I brought with my diabolic hands to your late father-in-law one white lamb, half-dead! Your… Helen! Your beloved beautiful Helen, sister of your present wife Alexandra…"

"Moments, how you slaughter time and you throw it in front of us like autumn leaves!" I shouted.

"I, I, I killed her, your Helen, Mr Constantine!…"

"Stop it, Mitros, stop it…"

"I am not going to stop until I say it all! You do whatever you want with me! Go to the police, to the judges! I don't care anymore! It is enough for me to redeem myself!… I killed Costoulas, the landowner's sun! I. I killed Helen as well. And I killed you too…"

"Erinyes who brought him here, tighten up to your coffins! What am I supposed to do with him now?" I shouted with a voice that was coming out of my guts like fire.

"Listen to me! Listen to me so that I can somehow start feeling lighter. I was a slave, a shepherd of the landowner Costoulas. John was tarnished by the hatred he was feeling for you. His hatred grew after Alexandra's refusal to start a 'relationship' with him. I took the love letter, hoping that I could save him. He asked for my help and I offered it to him like Judas for a bit of money."

"Erinyes, friends of justice, that you brought him in front of me like a worm! Tell me, tell me, what to do with him now…" I shouted again.

"Should I go on, hopefully I will feel lighter somehow, Mr Constantine?" he asked. "Only if he took you out of his way he would be saved. The man was mad! Your life was going to end at the rocks! And the plan was put to action. You were going to the rocks in the morning to take the lamb I was bringing. The whole night before I was plotting so that the plan would be successful. You see, the devils wait for the night! I would shake the big rock in such a way, that as soon as you stepped forward, while I was throwing the big stone, you would fall from the cliff! But you see, the opposite happened! You saved yourself and John and your Helen fell. You were dizzy from the height and you don't remember anything. While the big rock broke and you were about to fall with it, John, who was behind you, lost his balance and fell from the cliff! Helen ran towards you screaming your name, thinking that you were the one that is falling, slipped and fell from the cliff. But you were lucky! John died at the spot. Helen lasted until we brought her home. I brought her back on my hands! She was screaming your name all the time! Just before she died, steps before the front door of the house, she left her 'last will' to her father, who was screaming heartbroken, looking at the skies and hitting his chest. I remember as if it happened today what Helen said: "Constantine should marry Alexandra. The rocks, the rocks…" and then she died!"

"Where are you, you sweet soul to hear about your loss! But you know it… The pities cannot stand the darkness. They want light even though it is their death! So, towards the top, catch the 'alastor'[1]. But what are you going to do with him? He is always in the dark," I shouted broken-heartedly with all the strength I had left in my heart…

"I do feel my soul a bit lighter." said Mitros. "The smokes have disappeared. I can die now. I believe that earth can accept me now…"

"Miasmas, why do you run around to contaminate the world? You should kneel down and turn your eyes to somewhere else. To the earth that eats it…"

"…Is it going to eat me now, Mr Constantine?" he asked.

"You can be sure, Mitros! Please leave me alone now. The repentance has a bigger value than the good deed." I said.

"Mr Constantine, can you forgive me now?" asked Mitros.

"You have been punished enough, Mitros. The punishment of the conscious is the worst one! The repentance is the key that opens its prison. Go to the sheep now, Alcmaeon! The rocks, the rocks, I haven't forgotten."

"I will leave now, when I became an innocent bird. The ravines are going to stop looking like open graves to me, the springs - voices of werewolves and the streams - carcasses. I am leaving now, Mr Constantine…"

"Just a moment, Mitros." I told him. "I am waiting for the mayor. We are going to discuss the property of Costoulas, if I understood well from the half-words he was telling me. Anyway, I will tell him that I will share the property I bought from Costoulas between thirty landless families. To you, I will give ten acres close to the rocks. And the rocks will be knocked down!"

"Thank you, thank you, you are so very kind to take care of the sinful slaves. I am going now to the trees so that I can go take a breath…" he said and he left running…

"Good luck…"

---

1 Alastor. *A daemonic being that was creating calamity either itself or by possessing humans. In the latter case, the human himself that did the infamous or the vindictive act was named alastor, as it happened in the case of Orestes who killed his mother. Later on the* word became a generic type of insult for people that are mean and vile.

CHAPTER ELEVEN

Helen's notebook - an eternal hymn of love

The nights that were stirring my soul with their cycles, they couldn't stop me from reaching the end. And even though they were seeding dust that kills the grass, I was keeping my circle where the dust couldn't reach. It passed in front of me and in its stirring it buried itself. The unquenchable grave cannot show life. Death grows and those that were feeding from its tasteless juices to make cream as well. How can the life-bringing butterflies there? What can the honey-making bees suck from there? You night-sucking aurora, show me with light how the strength is not in the heights, since you in your veils are dragging it and you are throwing it in the waves and it trembles. I met it in the gulf only in the shades. But its voice was real. I found a solution in the shade of the ravine. The rocks equal death! Hence, the rocks had to die. Time established the voice and it on its turns - the lie that was hiding one addition to the stones. It was the same voice that I could always hear in the bay. And now I came closer to the spring that was singing only hymns in its land, a stone staircase with the musical key of love!

My thoughts stopped. They stopped and they passed above the rocks so that they can see from above what the deaf cliffs were hiding. Now I can see him coming. He is not alone! He pulled life from the rocks and presented it in my hands. Am I going to be able to hold it myself? But how dry time is! I have to keep her somewhere. Tell me, thoughts, where? You, that walk with her, where should I keep her? In an iron safe[1]? But time is throwing shovels, rusty shovels!

I opened Helen's notebook. My thought replied! To you, to you that in helicon the Muses fed you, to you I leave life! It doesn't die with her! I can hear her, I can hear her:

"Constantine, if death takes my body away, tell me, tell me, dear, are you going to take my soul?"

"Darling, death is only a flesh eater, and we people are the soul eaters!"

"I will not leave you, darling, to the soul rippers that will dig your soul with their beaks!"

"To you, my darling, I gave a talisman, so that you can have it next to your soul!"

"What a clear voice, what a sweet voice that the rocks can hear! What if they understand it? They hear only one voice, the one of the eagles with the crooked nails! But I will shout again, so that my soul can hear me…

The breasts
of one mother
were feeding us
at the croups of Pegasus.
What if the crows
down there
are sharpening their beaks
in the dry breasts
of earth!
We passed by the wind
the clouds cut in two
and the hoofs
turned into never setting starts.
What if the crows
down there
are burying themselves
in the hoofs of the Centaurs.
The breasts
of one mother

were feeding us up there on the Helicon[2]."

What a happiness in the land of the daffodils! Only one thought remained. And it turned into a song. Only one word blossomed and only it survived! Love…

The idol turned into haze. All that is left is thought. What fast winds push the haze and it becomes more beautiful? For the bogus their word faded, because it was only a pillow for the weight of the flesh. They forget that love is only a pillow for the soul!

Daffodils, daffodils

please hang

of my soul the lyre.

Some bird knocks her chords in the notebook with her poems. I am reading again some of them that Helen told me about:

"Dear, tell me that forever, as long as the rocks exist and even when they are knocked down, when the days become longer and shorter, and in the clouds and winters, we will always be together in the land of the daffodils!"

"A pillow of my soul, how your indestructible words are stabbing the wind. We are only in love. It is not our fault that other people have falsified the word with the water of the flesh and we leave the table of love drunk?"

"My love, is it true that one kiss waters love?"

"No," I had replied to her back then, as she had written down in her notebook:

"The lyre is ringing, my love, the lyre that hanged in the land of the daffodils." she had written down with black letters!

"You are right, Constantine. I heard its music in the daffodils! I called it 'happiness'!"

Yes, I gave her the music of the beats of the unwatered soul, as clean as

your lyre!
To her, who gave
the love in my hands!

At first it was only a thought. I collected its prophecies. I guessed her death at the rocks. I guessed from the voices of the eagles that were surrounding her. I heard her voice. Her voice always echoes. Isn't it a prophecy?

"Constantine, if death takes my body away, tell me, tell me, dear, are you going to take my soul?"

How could I, daffodils, tell me, how could I live without her soul?
Daffodils, daffodils
please hang
of my soul the lyre.
A bird is playing on its chords!

The rocks need to die. It was the voice that I could always hear in the valley. The sun is always slipping down in its chasm. My sun is always raising up in the temple of my heart. Who could stop its route? But I never have night. Mine is not a dream. My idol is true, it is reality. The rocks need to die…

---

1 Safe (kasa). *The word is used as "coffin" in some region of Greece.*

2 Helicon. *A mountain famous in the Greek mythology because in it there were two springs dedicated to the Muses: Aganippe and Hippocrene. Hesiod mentioned other springs that were homes of the Muses.*

CHAPTER TWELVE

A school made from stone from the rocks

Something like steps becomes alive on the cobbled stones. Can it be steps from the land of the past? I hear a voice:

"Mrs Alexandra, Mr Constantine!"

I got up.

"Good evening, Mr Ostas, good evening."

"How are you Mr Nikos, how are you, Mr Bekos?" my wife Alexandra greets him.

"Let's say alright," said Mr Nikos. "Ah, what does the old human go through until he dies!"

"Sit down, Mr Bekos. I was waiting for you."

"Yes, I had informed you that I was coming. Am I bothering you, Professor?"

"Please, call me Constantine."

"It is a bit difficult for me, but I will try. Whatever you want, Sir…"

"The same again! I said no Mr and Sir."

"It just came out. But how can I speak to you like this, you and your big personality, Mr Constantine."

"These are formalities. What matters is the essence."

"Ah, when did twelve years pass by from then, Constantine. Twelve years, like it was yesterday since I found you at the rocks, under the big spring… When I remember those unfairly lost children, I get mad!"

I didn't say anything. What else could I say? Mr Nikos was now the mayor of the village - he had really passed by the rocks back then I was impressed by his softness, the innocence of his soul, his wise words…

"I remember, I remember that image as if it was yesterday, Mr Nikos. I cannot put it out of my brain!"

"Ah, the beautiful Helen! Ah, poor John! How many poisons you left behind you? Poor Constantine, where is your Helen? I wish you all the best, Constantine! You are worth it. I am happy to see you. Our village is talking big about you!"

"Thank you, Mr Nikos. I have always admired you. What can we offer you? Alexandra, Alexandra, where are you, my heart?"

"Excuse me, Mr mayor. I went out for a second to bring back my daughter Helen from the springs. She was playing with the water and her clothes are all soaking wet." said Alexandra.

"Please, Alexandra, bring to the mayor whatever he wants."

"I would like a lemonade." said Mr Nikos.

"Mr Nikos is our friend, he wouldn't misunderstand." said Alexandra.

"Do whatever you are supposed to, my child, don't worry." answered Mr Nikos.

"So, Mr mayor." I said.

"Constantine, I came to ask you about something that according to my opinion is very good for the village. I would like you to help me. I know that you can. I thought that you would always want to help Costoulas' village."

"Whatever you want." I replied.

"We were thinking about the following," he went on. "As you know, Costoulas in his last will left half of his property to the church and the other half to the community. He was also saying that it can be sold only if with the money gets invested for something good for the village. You know. You bought the ravine from us as soon as we informed you last year, when we came to Athens for the bidding contest for Costoulas' property that he left to the community. And you also bought every acre at a very high price."

"Ah, it's alright. I wanted to buy it on high price, so that I can help you."

"Thank you, Constantine! Now when you came back to the village - how many years haven't you come back?"

"Five years! But before I left straight away."

"Yes, five years! Where was I? Ah yes, I remembered. Now when you came to the village, I thought about asking you a favour. To help the village… We have collected some money. Costoulas - God forgive him - is a benefactor of our village. We thought about building a village, so that the generations can remember him. You know that we don't have a school for our children and there is no way that the government will build one for us. Because our money is not enough, I would like to ask you, Constantine, to help us…"

"Of course, Mr mayor!" I replied happily. "This would make me really happy. I am at your disposition. Whatever you want and as much as you want. You can start even from tomorrow…"

"Thank you very much, Mr Ostas! The village will be always grateful for your help!"

"It's my duty, Mr mayor, it is my responsibility to the place where I grew up!"

"You have always been a good person. And this is why you flourished…"

"Don't start now all the sweet political words…"

"No, no! They are coming out of my heart! You were a poor as a child. However, you had the desire and the strength to keep walking inspire of the obstacles. And you are the first university professor that has ever come out of this village! The late Mr Vassilis, your father-in-law, he was dying from his suffering for Helen - he was always talking about you: "I lost my

Helen, but God gave me Constantine."

Flooded by excitement and with a knot in my throat, a big teardrop rolled down my cheek.The mayor saw me and said excitedly:

"Constantine, I know that I am stabbing you in the soul with all that talk. But the words are coming out of my heart freely… Please forgive me…"

"It's ok, mayor. I want to ask you that the school gets built with stone from the rocks. I will knock down the rocks, I will flatten them!"

"Well, is there a better quality stone for building than the one at the rocks? I understand… The rocks need to be knocked down, Constantine…"

"I won't leave even a pebble, mayor. The rocks will become a garden!"

"Of course! And I will erect a statue of Helen!"

"No, I will, just like the one in my soul."

"Alright, alright. Than we will make one of John in the school yard."

"No, I will do this as well. You will give the school the name of Costoulas as a benefactor. It should be like this…"

"And what about your name?" he asked.

"No, no! Don't mention anything about me! I thought about something else as well. Tomorrow is the twelfth anniversary of Helen's death. I decided on this occasion to divide the ravine that I bought between the landless of the village. You can regulate that. From tomorrow we should start our work. You will give ten acres to Mitros. The area around the rocks I will keep. All the rest, you should divide correctly and fairly. Make sure no one has complaints…"

"Ah, Constantine, the world is greedy and ungrateful. As much as you give it, is always complaining. But this is something I didn't expect! When a place gives birth to such a person, what is there that the person can fear?"

"… It's stoning, Mr mayor, it's stoning! No one is a prophet in their own village!"

"You are right. We are going to hear a lot. How he wants to 'eat' money with the mayor, how they will settle their own people, how money goes to money. Slyness and lies. If you knew what some people say about me!"

"Bravo, Constantine!" said Alexandra, as a tear, full with pain and joy at the same time was slowly running down her cheek. "I was expecting a lot from you, but not this!" she added.

"Happiness, love and joy in the land of the daffodils, Alexandra!" I said.

"I wish you to be always well, Constantine!" she said excitedly.

"Well, I am leaving now." said the mayor. "Tomorrow the ravine will echo from the machines. Soon the rocks will be dead! Goodnight and thank you." said Mr Nikos and left.

"Goodnight, mayor. All the best." I said.

CHAPTER THIRTEEN

Consignments in Helen's notebook

And you, my West, my love, my memory whose incense attacks my thoughts, you will always remember the dawns. How many times do you stay for a bit on the cushion of the mountain, to hear a lullaby from her lips. Her lips were throwing your rays in my mouth. And then you stood there to throw your last thoughts into her soul, such a moment, your eyes were throwing sparks in the darkness! You are always bringing these hours, you put in front of me her eternal words, her voice, the voice of my joy!

"Constantine, if death takes my body away, tell me, tell me, dear, are you going to take my soul?"

"My dear, my love, I will keep your soul as a talisman forever together with mine!"

And now when I am digging into the poems, Apollo is a prophet! I heard your stern song, my love. I predicted your loss, your death at the rocks! There I sow the prophecies. The dolphins will only remind us of the dawns! Her stern song that the sunset wants to hear! The song that echoed before her death, so that death could come spreading only arrows to the frog-people. Now when I am digging into her poems, I find prophecies in her words:

Stern song,

my stern nightingale,

in the stern hour of the day,

before you roost

to the feathery cypress over there,

tell me!

Stern song,

my lyre

before the chords

a fence

of my dry garden I will make,

tell me.

Stern song,

of the eternal taste of my garden

- when it is useless to the living! -

cut the lemon blossoms

and nest

in the lonely cypress

over there

and tell me!

Look, look,

how over there is a garden

full with cypresses

in the middle

and it bends as if it's calling

a soul

so that it dies as well!

And then when your words tore apart the veil of the night, on your altar, I spreaded the pieces of my soul that you are holding tight.

When you don't have anything else

to offer for a sacrifice

offer your altar!

All these, my darling, were epitaph flutterings. The harvester ploughed in May and scattered a light yellow colour in the ravine. But I am not a harvester! I was a prophet. I am not a vintager! I was a collector. To me the vintager just gave the fruits he collected and left the leaves for the autumn.

That harvester ploughs my May. Death resurrects in such times. Twelve hours, twelve years, twelve centuries come together at one place where they erect the altar of one value, one faith different from the one that they build and knock down so that they can dust the people. The big destroyers! There on the top, pieces of my thoughts I saved and they created happiness. Happiness was built on top of the altar, happiness that uncovered them, anyway, the immovable of one belief in the beautiful, the ideal, the good, with these eternal words that are carved in the altar I offered, it will fly in the skies.

When you don't want to lose

the beautiful,

show how you want it when it's lost!

I offered my altar so that I can keep the happiness that flows from the eternal human river. Happiness is a conclusion, it destroys hope. When there is hope, happiness flatters without finding a branch to sit. I called it to sit on the altar I offered. I saw it. So that I can hope. Why should I wait?

The flowers, the roses

I uprooted

-and they had also nails-

to see what roots

the worms are gonna eat!

My fence

will not let May in anymore

to hear the songs

of my lyre.

Let it go over there

to see it hanging on the cypress!

In your root

soul-born,

I will let my soul

- the garden died -

to sprinkle it

with autumn drops.

Stern song,

stern gift,

my lyre without chords

in your grave!

My death will give

height to your cypress!

It looks like death needs to die so that humanity will be born and in its branches - happiness and joy. The voice brought me its meaning. It told me about some flattening, it showed me some settling, showed me its height. The rocks give birth to death! This is why they have to die! How Golgotha's stubbles were all empty and its top was full of dead bodies? Only one garden was holding Life in the grave. How many were crucified and resurrected? Only the truth! Only the statue of the resurrection knocked down fake idols that were covered with its dust!

The rocks were feeding from the dryness hit by the sun, they were grabbing you. But the night, that was closing inside itself happiness and love made you a light idol. This shows truth. And you told me then that May was imagining dream colours in its petals.

"Constantine, please tell me, darling, if death catches the body, tell me, my love, are you going to catch my soul?"

The cross becomes sacred

by the blood of the robbers!

This is what you told me. These words are going to remind me the twilights while they are darkening the empty sky and show the stone teeth of the rocks, ready to tear apart the steps of the prophet, to hide their shadows of every voice of joy and to strengthen the voice of the eagle, of hatred.

My dear, in the land of the daffodils I had spread hope and expectance. The harvester offered me happiness! What else could he give me? Even though you died together with the vines and the dry grass, you died to offer me the fruit. This is the fruit I was searching on the earth. This is what I was waiting for. Now in the daffodils I put the fruit so that I can show you how the crows are flying only over the dead bodies. It belongs only to the Zephyrs. Every soul moved by the body rests in the daffodils. Every body that was suffocated by the soul, is offered to the crows.

It was one prophecy that was chasing me for years. I could never escape from it! And if Castalia dries out, where will the nightingales drink water from? My only joy is to remain standing at your grave, holding your soul. This shows that there is something in the newly digged graves that were sealed forever. In between the fake altars, there is one real! This one the humans hadn't noticed because it was high. Only in the fake altars leans the weight of the flesh that suffocated and, in the end, melts…

Remind me, West, remind me the altars covered by flesh. I find them when the wind of the memories opens her notebook:

Tasteless flesh, unholy hands,

the first sacrifice

of a deadly taste,

to which dead

-there is no one alive anymore!-

gifts, Greeks, to bear!

The smell of myrrh

from the bowels of Castalia

you brought

and the prophecy of Pythia

to my bowels

- there is no altar anymore.

Where is it, sweet eternity, the altar?

Before the victory,
or after the victory of whom.
In the flow of your poetry
which altar covered with flesh
hollows the crows?

The rocks tonight are counting the hours that will never come back. A circle is closing. This shows only that many other circles are covering the rays of the circle of life. Only when the rocks are gone, in the temple of the soul, the light arrow of happiness will show. Then even the chests of the eagles will get destroyed and the Harpies will run away from the land of the daffodils, from every land that they have erected and still erect altars, not for sacrifice with smoke to fake Gods, but to the power of love and happiness that holds the human above the things, above the darkness and the haze…

And then, the rocks were a mass that was hiding with its shadow the weak ones. But the voice from the bay and before and after was calling me to turn off their shadow. I now understood my chariot.

I had to keep walking, because only this means strength!

I was dreaming only about one land. The land of the daffodils, with one aurora that was showing me the meaning of darkness. Then the rocks were shrieking and squeaking. I collected all my thoughts and I offered them under the same vine in the garden of the cottage, I spread them in the yard. And when in the evening those poems were heard, than Love happened! And then I gave to it as a gift what made me stronger: my eternal song for it! When the rocks were spreading their terror, our poems destroyed the fear.

I was dragging my expectation then to the ravine and I knew, I knew that the good and the beautiful have been tortured. And then the dawn showed me the twilight, gave food to my thoughts, stopped me there, standing in the soil so that I can look the sky, stuck the rays of my eyes to the clouds, strengthened my steps to the road to the rocks.

I had to keep walking, because only this means strength!

I could hear a voice coming from the vine full with fruits, as I was staring at the rocks:

Show how beautiful something is by dying for it!

I had to keep walking, because only this means strength!

If the lie was wearing the shape of truth, the strength has undressed it! The voice from the ravine is just a weep, we are stone masses and the nights are sucking the human happiness. The escape turns into a graveyard of ourselves and the lie- a cypress on our graves.

I had to keep walking, because only this means strength!

But, we have to always stand in the ravine so that we can always hear the voice of truth. Always, there is one way that brings us to the land of the daffodils. Always there is a life that is looking for the real life and the real happiness!

And always those two are in the hands of life!

However,

the flames of hell

are around us

when we are still

in paradise!

With these poems Helen's notebook ends. A sacred camel, a sacred censer with eternal hymns to love and happiness.

The notebook of my Helen… This eternal hymn we should sing, as Lamartine used to say…

THE END

DIMITRIS L. STERGIOU

Dimitris is a journalist and author of many books, mainly on economics, folklore and linguistics. This novel is an unique literary book.

He is born in Palaiomanina, Aitoloakarnania, to parents who worked as farmers. He completed his primary education at the Palaiomanina Elementary School and his secondary education at the Palamaiki School of Iera Polis in Mesologgi. As a top high-school student, he quickly became the flag bearer of his institution. In 1961, he graduated as the first in his high-school class and continued his university studies (in politics, economics and, later, philosophy) in Athens, on a scholarship.

From 1966 to 1970, he was a member of the Editorial Board of the magazine "Trapeziki Oikonomotechniki Epitheorisis" (Bank Logistics Review) and an analyst at the homonymous "Oikonomotechniko Kentro" (Logistics Centre). At the beginning of 1970, he was hired at Lampraki Publishing Group as an editor of "Oikonomikos Tachydromos" (Financial Courier) and the newspapers "Vima" and "Nea". In 1979, he became the Chief Editor and, later, Editorial Director of "Oikonomikos Tachydromos". He was a member, columnist and analyst at the newspapers "Nea", "Vima" and "Sunday Vima" until 2001.

In 2001, he was transferred to "Sunday Eleftheros Typos", initially as a publishing consultant and editorial director, and later as a manager. He left his position at "Sunday Eleftheros Typos" in October 2003 and was transferred to "Apogevmatini" as Editorial Director. Since his retirement, he has been involved with the publishing house Stergiou Limited in the UK, and has authored a variety of books.

In 1997, along with many of his fellow villagers, he cofounded the cultural society "Society of Friends of the Palaiomanina Monuments", in order to preserve, highlight and capitalise on the rich cultural heritage and tradition of his village. So far, the results have been promising.

Now, he is running his own Publications with his daughters Eleni and Artemis Eleftheria.

He is also a member of the Athens Union of Journalists in Daily Newspapers. He is married to Nota and has four children, Leonidas, Nikos, Eleni and Artemis – Eleutheria, as well as two grandchildren, Nota – Theodora and Christina – Konstantina.

His books

He has received multiple awards from various bodies and organisations, and he has authored numerous books:

• "Transcripts from the rebellion of '21 in Akarnania". Athens 1971 (sold out).

• "The Rocks" (novel), A hymn to human, eternal values and institutions. Filippoti Publishing, Athens 1992 (sold out).

• "Twenty Lost Years" (The chronicles of the pillaging of Greek Economy during the period 1972 – 1992). Papazisi Publishing, Athens 1994.

• "Palaiomanina from the depths of time to today". Self-published, Athens 1996 (sold out).

• "Tis Sofokleous to Kagkelo" (The twelve "bear and bull" stock exchange cycles from 1972 to September 1999 – lessons and findings). Papazisi Publishing, Athens 2000 (multiple reissues).

• "This is Greece" (the 8 greatest crimes in economy after the political changeover). Ellinika Grammata Publishing, Athens 2001.

• "Customs of Vlachoi in Palaiomanina, deriving in ancient Greece". D. Papadima Publishing, Athens 2001.

• "The Big Bubble of Greek Economy, 1981 – 2001". Papazisi Publishing, Athens 2002.

• "The Big Bubble of Modernisation by K. Simitis". Papazisi Publishing, Athens 2004.

• "The political drama of Greece, 1981 – 2005" (preface by ex – Prime Minister Konstantinos Mitsotakis). Papazisi Publishing, Athens 2005.

• "Dictionary. 4,500 Mycenaean, Homeric, Byzantine and Modern Greek roots in the speech of Vlachoi". D.Papadima Publishing, Athens 2007.

• "The Losers. How they destroyed Greek economy and plundered Greek households", ebook. Production by LeonMedia MEPE, Halandri 2011.

• "For prison" – Documents – indictments against the politicians who destroyed the economy and our country during the past thirty years, Ebook. Stergiou Limited, London 2012-2013.

• Greek Culture –Over 800 ancient Greek words in the speech of Greek Vlachoi. Stergiou Limited, London 2012.

• Half Century of "Greek Statistics". A brief but revealing tour of the main financial figures of Greek economy from 1961 to today. Greek edition: Stergiou Limited, London 2012 – 2013 – English edition: Stergiou Limited – Amazon.co.uk, London 2012-2013.

• How would Greek economy be if… The relation between financial and real economy, with specific examples, studies, tables and numbers. Stergiou Limited, London 2013.

• Bank-nourished State and State-nourished Banks – A disastrous relation for Greece. Stergiou Limited, London 2013.

• I, the Fool. The tragic story of 33 closures from 1978 to today, at the expense of taxpayers and in favour of tax evaders.

• Stories of Financial Madness 1974 – 2008. Stergiou Limited, London 2013.

DEVID J. FRANCO

David is a freelance music composer with over 10 years experience producing music in the video games industry. His work has featured on titles published by Warner Bros. THQ, Square Enix and Konami as well as on national television in the US, UK and Australia.

The game audio veteran David J. Franco and former Sony Marketing Manager Dominic Parris founded in 2012 the Melodynamix® to pound out high fidelity, ear-catching, critic-aweing OSTs across a variety of genres for interactive media.

www.ingramcontent.com/pod-product-compliance
Lightning Source LLC
Chambersburg PA
CBHW071019180726
48291CB00004B/1534